C000076319

He Can Move the Mountains

Mountains of Faith, Book 2

Catherine Barbey

Copyright © 2020 by Catherine Barbey

All rights reserved.

Any unauthorised reprint or use of this material is prohibited. No part of this book may be reproduced, stored, or transmitted in any form or by any means, electronic, mechanical, photocopying, recording, or otherwise, without the written permission of the author, except for the use of brief quotations in a book review.

Scripture taken from the Holy Bible, NEW INTERNATIONAL VERSION®, NIV® Copyright © 1973, 1978, 1984, 2011 by Biblica, Inc.® Used by permission. All rights reserved worldwide.

This book is a work of fiction. Names, characters, organisations, places, and events are either the product of the author's imagination or used fictitiously. Any resemblance to actual persons, living or dead, is purely coincidental and not intended by the author. Locales, persons, or events already in the public domain are used fictitiously.

Cover Art by Rebecca Priestley
Cover Design by Rob Richards

For more from Catherine Barbey join her mailing list
at catherinebarbey.com/readerslist

Dedicated to my family,
each of whom played a valuable role
in helping bring this book into existence.

List of Characters

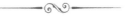

Bela and Michael, with Angelina - their adopted
     daughter.
Aslan and Radima - Bela's parents.
Azamat - Bela's older brother.
Madina - Bela's older sister.
Milana - Azamat's former girlfriend.
Alikhan - Milana's son.
Murat - Milana's husband.
Musa - Madina's ex-husband.
Alyona - Madina and Musa's daughter, and Bela and
     Azamat's niece.
Oleg - Madina's boss at work.
Lida - Radima's cousin, married to Vladimir. They have
     a son, Daniel, and a daughter, Irina.
Pavel - Aslan's son with his former mistress, Maria.
Zalina - Angelina's mother and Bela's best friend, who
     died in the Beslan tragedy along with her husband
     and son.

Glossary

Apteka - a chemist or pharmacy
Babushka - an elderly lady or grandmother
Circassians - an indigenous people group of the
        North Caucasus
Dom Pionerov - a large, municipal building,
        formerly used by the national Pioneers
        organisation
Kasha - porridge
Kolbasa - salami
Lapochka - a term of endearment, meaning
        something like 'dear one'
Marshroutka - a mini-bus operating like a bus but
        able to drop passengers where they request
        as long as it's along the route
Shawarma - a sandwich wrap of Middle Eastern
        origin, usually filled with meat, lettuce and
        mayonnaise
Smetana - sour cream
Tyotya - aunt or auntie

Prologue

July 2010, Pavel

Pavel emerged from the shadows and quickened his step, keeping the hood of his sweatshirt pulled down low over his face. He could feel his heart beating faster inside his chest, and he wiped his sweaty palms on the legs of his jeans before placing them back inside his sweatshirt pockets. His hands met something cold and hard, and a rush of adrenaline flooded through his body. This was it. The moment he'd been waiting for.

He'd been here in the Caucasus, in the town of Shekala, for two months now, planning and observing and waiting. Once or twice, waking up cold from his night on the park bench, he'd thought about going back home to Moscow and had almost given in, but then he'd forced himself to remember his mother's face. Her pale, thin, lined face. Her bloodshot eyes betraying a drug addiction she was barely keeping under control; her thin, creased mouth that had smoked too many cigarettes and drunk too many shots of vodka.

No matter how hard he tried, he couldn't

remember her happy, but she had been once. The old photos she kept in a drawer in their run-down apartment portrayed a beautiful, adventurous woman. Well-dressed and attractive. That had been when they lived in Shekala, but he couldn't remember that. They had moved to Moscow when he was only four. It had been just the two of them for as long as he could remember, not including the shadows of strange men flitting in and out of their apartment, each one staying less time than the one before.

He remembered clearly, though, the day when she'd first told him about his father. He'd been about eleven, very ill and in hospital, and his mother had been anxious and troubled as the hospital bills started piling up. But then one day she'd arrived at his bedside looking jubilant and full of hope.

"It's going to be alright, Pavlik, love!"

"How, Mama? What do you mean? Am I getting better?"

"You will, darling, you will. We can pay the doctors now, and they'll make you better."

Pavel had looked at her, confused. They'd had very little money all his life, just scraping by, really. "Where has the money come from, Mama? Do you have a new job?"

"No, no." She'd leaned over and squeezed his hand, her eyes shining. "He's going to help us. Your father. He's finally going to look after you, Pavlik."

His father.

Pavel crossed the street and entered the town park. The man ahead was walking briskly, his briefcase swinging at his side. He'd worked late tonight, the man from the fancy office buildings, and the dark seemed to make him nervous. And so it should.

Pavel had caught glimpses of this man over the last two months. A rich, self-important, pompous individual who worked in some high-level position in the local government. Pavel scowled and swore quietly under his breath. This man lived in a nice house with a nice-looking family. Did he ever spare a thought for his other son and the woman he'd tossed aside? If he'd done the right thing and looked after them properly then he and his mother would never have had to live in squalor in a bare, dirty apartment in a rough part of Moscow. He wouldn't have had to endure beatings from the local neighbourhood gang of boys, or rummage through the trash trying to find scraps of edible food. Anger filled Pavel's body and gave his stride a new determination as he followed the man at a distance. His mother could have had a happy life. The men, the alcohol, the drugs: none of that would have been necessary if this lowlife had stepped up and done his duty. The two-faced coward!

A small voice flitted into Pavel's mind. *"He did pay your hospital bills. You might have died. He wouldn't have let you die."* Pavel brushed the voice aside. The money had stopped completely once he'd been pronounced well and allowed home, and his mother hadn't seen a single rouble since.

The man had reached the dark part of the park now. A couple of the street lamps were broken, thanks to Pavel's good aim with a handful of stones a week or so ago. This was it. This was the moment he'd been rehearsing in his mind for weeks. He broke into a run and the man whipped around, his eyes large and white with panic. They were face to face at last. Father and son.

"What do you want?" The man's voice was loud but shaky. He looked around nervously, but there was no one there. No one to help.

"You don't recognise me, do you?" Pavel sneered. He pulled the hood off his head. Let him get a good look. Would he see the resemblance? Would he feel sorry for the son he'd abandoned? He hated this man with every fibre of his being. He stared him in the eye, but the man just looked confused.

"No, who are you? What do you want?" he repeated, taking a couple of steps backwards.

Pavel laughed a cold, shallow laugh. "Revenge. This is for my mother, Maria. This is for the life you took from her. A life for a life."

He reached into his pocket and drew out the gun. The Glock 17 felt light and familiar and he sure knew how to use it. At least his gruelling military service had been good for something. The man's face turned an ashen shade of white, his eyes widened in terror and he turned as if to run, but Pavel grabbed his arm. The briefcase fell to the floor and burst open, scattering a ream of paper along the terracotta paving slabs that tiled the walkway.

A shout rang out. Pavel flinched and looked up. Someone was running towards them. Someone had seen them. This wasn't supposed to happen, this wasn't part of the plan. It was late and dark, who could have spotted them? He swore loudly and turned back to look at his father. He hadn't come all this way or suffered so much to let this chance go.

He pulled the trigger.

It was a hasty shot, straight into the man's stomach. He could have aimed better, but he'd had no time to think now. He turned and ran as fast as he could, back in the direction he'd come. He didn't look back, but he heard his father groan and slump to the floor. The other man ran faster, but his footsteps stopped when he reached Pavel's father and didn't follow after Pavel himself. Had he got away with it? He ran as fast as he could, the gun still in his hand. His body was pumped with adrenaline and his heart was simultaneously full of jubilation and shock.

He had done it.

He had had revenge at last.

1

He moves mountains

without their knowing it...

Job 9:5

Chapter 1

One week earlier, Bela

Bela placed the bag of groceries on the floor just inside the doorway and bent down to remove her sandals. She chose her favourite pair of summer slippers and then looked over to see if Angelina needed any help with her shopping bag.

"Don't worry, I can manage, *Tyotya* Bela" said the ten-year-old, puffing a little as she came through the door.

Bela took the bag from her. "I do hope they're going to mend the lift soon. It's not much fun dragging shopping bags up four flights of stairs in this heat."

"Tell me about it!" Angelina rolled her eyes slightly as she lifted her leg up to remove her shoes. This eye rolling thing was becoming a habit, Bela noted. Her little girl was growing up. Of course, Angelina wasn't really her little girl. She and Michael had adopted her five years ago after Angelina's parents and older brother had been killed in the terrorist attack at the school in Beslan. Bela shuddered. Even now, nearly six years after the tragedy, she was still traumatised by the horrible memories, seeing all the suffering on the television and not knowing until several days later that her best friend, Zalina, Angelina's mother, had died in the attack. Fortunately, Angelina herself hadn't remembered much from that day. Even her own 'First Bell' at school, three years ago, hadn't triggered any memories and had passed without any concern on her part, despite the wrestling going on inside Bela to hold back her own tears and pretend to be nothing but happy and joyful instead for Angelina's sake. She still worried about whether the trauma was deeply buried and would surface as Angelina grew older and came across more information on the internet. It was something that she and Michael prayed regularly about.

There I go again, God, worrying as usual, and letting past hurts spoil our present moments. You gave Angelina to us to look after, and I trust you to heal her wounds when the time is right. Just, please give her a happy childhood.

"Can I watch TV now?" Angelina asked eagerly. "Not until you've helped me unpack the groceries, *lapochka*." Bela smiled but her eyes were firm. Angelina might be growing up in an apartment in town, but she still needed to learn how to help out around the place. Bela's own childhood, growing up in the village of Awush, just a couple of miles away, had been full of chores, especially in the summer. There had been the vegetables to plant, weed and harvest, and the fruit trees and bushes to tend to. Not to mention having to look after the cow and the chickens.

"I think I'll get another crate of tomatoes from the market tomorrow. We need to do some more bottling," Bela mumbled to herself.

"Really? We did a whole load last week,"

Angelina protested as she put the tins away in the cupboard.

"My Nana…"

"Here we go again with the Nana story!" Angelina interrupted, laughing.

Bela laughed too. "Sorry, do I go on about her a lot?"

"Yes! But that's okay. She was special, I understand that. Like mine." The smile disappeared from Angelina's face, and she continued to unpack the shopping bags more thoughtfully.

Bela touched her lightly on the shoulder. "Yes, your grandmother was a very special lady too." Angelina had lived with her grandmother since she was born, and Rosa, her grandmother, had protected her all through the Beslan affair, begging Bela to adopt the little girl before she was no longer able to look after her anymore. Bela felt a pang of regret again that Rosa hadn't lived long enough to know that Bela had abided by Zalina's last wishes and taken Angelina to be her own. She'd hesitated too long. She'd still been grieving the tragic loss of her best friend, and confused over her relationship with Michael, so that by the time she'd made the right decision Angelina had been living in the local orphanage for four months already.

"What were you going to say about your Nana…?"

Bela's thoughts turned to her own grandmother. "My Nana would bottle at least fifty jars of tomatoes and fifty jars of cucumbers every summer to see us all through the winter. I want to pass down the tradition to you too, Angelina."

"Along with her secret recipe."

Bela laughed. "Yes, her not-so-secret-now recipe."

"There." Angelina closed the cupboard door. "Now can I watch TV?"

"Yes, sure." Bela watched Angelina race out of the kitchen, and soon the sounds of Angelina's favourite show came drifting through the apartment.

Bela unpacked the last of the groceries and put the shopping bags away. They didn't have many luxury items in the cupboards, but they had plenty to live on quite comfortably. Michael's grant from the university in England was small by British standards but stretched a long way here in the Caucasus. And there was her salary from Cody's tourism business too, where she worked as his personal assistant and office manager. She looked around at her small but cosy kitchen. *Thank you, God, you're so good to us!* She'd learned a long time ago that gratitude was the antidote to fear and anxiety. She allowed her mind to drift instead to the memories of her wedding day, and a large smile broke out over her face. She'd hesitated too about marrying her handsome British linguist, but along with adopting Angelina that had been one of the best decisions she'd ever made. The third, or probably the best decision of all, had been believing that Jesus was indeed the Way, the Truth and the Life, even down here in the Caucasus, and accepting Him into her heart.

Michael should be home soon. Perhaps she should check her phone, where was it? Bela walked into the hallway and fumbled around in her handbag for a few seconds before her fingers latched around the familiar, rectangular object she was seeking. Yes, there was a text from Michael. He planned to be home around six. That gave her plenty of time to fix some dinner for the three of them. Her eyes fell on the framed wedding photo on the shelf of the hallway cupboard unit. She picked it up, dusting the top a little and running her fingers over the glass. There they were, two of the happiest people in the world. Michael in his traditional English suit with tails and a top hat, and Bela in her traditional Circassian dress, with long flowing sleeves, a belt and embroidered bodice, and the tall hat with the soft, fine veil cascading down her shoulders and back. Two cultures colliding and yet somehow joining as one. Angelina was smiling up at both of them, her eyes sparkling with the same joy as theirs. She'd been a beautiful bridesmaid, this bonus daughter of hers. Michael had stepped effortlessly into the role of a father, and it was almost as if they'd always been together, their little family of three.

Bela put the picture back on the shelf, a stab of sadness piercing her heart.

Will we ever be a family of four, Lord? How long?

She ran the palm of her hand over her flat stomach, trying to imagine for a moment what it might feel like to have life swelling inside her. But she pulled her hand away. It wasn't going to happen. Not this month, certainly. Disappointment flooded through her soul again. She had to find something to make herself busy; something else to occupy her thoughts. The way she was learning to do month after frustrating month. They'd been married for four years already, but plenty of people had to wait this long, even longer, before they got pregnant, right? It didn't mean anything. It was just the way things were.

But doubt was growing in her mind. Is God really good to us? Does he really answer prayer? The exuberance of the first year or two after she'd become a Christian was fading, if she was honest, and now she was beginning to wonder again what it really meant to be a follower of Jesus. It certainly wasn't all flowers and sunshine, that's for sure. Michael always had wise words to say about these kinds of things. What was that verse he'd mentioned? *In this world you'll have trouble. But take heart for I have overcome the world.* Something like that. Being a Christian didn't shield you from pain and disappointment. But, why would God withhold this good thing from them? Why wasn't God answering their prayers?

Bela busied herself in the kitchen. She peeled and chopped the potatoes and put them in the frying pan, covering them with the lid. She added the chicken legs she'd just bought to another frying pan, and while they were cooking, she chopped up some fresh cucumbers and tomatoes, mixing them with *smetana* and dill to make a salad.

Right on cue, the key turned in the lock and Michael's face appeared around the kitchen door.

"Hi," he said, before wrestling his shoes off his feet.

"Hi Michael," Angelina's voice called out from the living room.

"Hey, sweet pea!" he called back. Bela heard him walk down the hallway toward the bedroom, and he returned a few minutes later dressed in more comfortable, cooler clothes.

"Phew, I still can't get used to this heat!" he said, wiping the sweat from his forehead and reaching for one of the glasses that Bela had just put out onto the table. He filled it with water from the filter. Bela had got used to his habit of drinking filtered water, even though she and her family had been quite happy to drink the water straight from the tap. Maybe he was right about the metals and the parasites, but it all tasted the same to her. Michael grabbed some ice cubes from the freezer and added them to the glass before sitting down. Even though it was past six o'clock, it was still stifling hot in the apartment, and he had placed himself with his back to the small, shuddery fan which was doing its best to shift cooler air towards the occupants of the room.

Bela was used to hot summers, but she had to admit that even she was still getting used to summers in town apartments. Out in the village it had seemed a little cooler in their larger rooms, and of course they'd had immediate access to a garden with shady apple trees. She'd moved into this apartment soon after adopting Angelina, and then Michael had joined them a year later, after they'd got married. There were advantages to living nearer to the centre of town, but she did miss the village and its slower, cooler pace of life.

She opened the kitchen window as far as it would go and sat down on the stool next to him. A trickle of sweat ran down the back of her neck. This was the hottest July she could remember. Michael took a big gulp of water, placed the glass back on the table and exhaled loudly.

"Is everything okay?" she asked. It was unusual to see him looking anxious, but she could guess what was on his mind. His concerns had been brewing for the past few weeks.

"I'm worried, Bela. I don't know what to do."

"You mean about your funding? I still don't understand how they can just stop your money like that."

"Education cuts. Everyone is suffering."

"But your three-year contract got renewed, didn't it?"

"Yes, but the actual amount of the research grant was never set in stone. They're not stopping the money, just reducing it. A lot."

"But you have other money?"

Michael sighed. "There's my trust fund, yes, but I

was hoping not to dip into that too much. I have our future to think of. Angelina's future too. I need to find a sustainable way of earning a living. You can't live off a trust fund for ever."

Bela picked up a nearby magazine and started fanning herself with it while she checked the status of the potatoes and chicken. She didn't know what to say. She didn't know how to help. She didn't understand the ins and outs of British academia.

"How much more do you think we need? I could try to get another job?" She sat back down at the table next to him.

Michael took her hand and kissed it. "You already work for Cody and I don't want you to do too much. I'll find a way. I just need to start applying for some jobs sooner than I was expecting, I guess."

Bela's heart fell. "What kind of jobs can you get here in the Caucasus, Michael?"

Michael looked at her, his eyes filled with sad understanding.

"I know I promised you we could stay here, in your homeland, Bela. But..."

"But you have temporary residency here. That's good for another year or two and then you can apply for permanent residency."

"I know, I know. It's not about the residency. I need to do something. I need to have a job. I need to provide for our family."

There was a pause, both of them, no doubt, thinking the same thing but not daring to mention it. Their growing family? Future children? Or just their little family of three?

Bela stood up to refill her own water glass. When she spoke, there was a bitterness to her voice which she couldn't cover up.

"So, you're going to apply for jobs in England?"

"I don't know, Bela. I don't know."

He stood up and took her hand, gently turning her towards him. Her resistance melted and she looked up into his face, accepting his kiss of reconciliation. A reminder that they were in this together as a couple. For better or for worse, wasn't that what she'd promised?

"We just need to keep praying that God will give us guidance, Bela. He's in control. He knows what He's doing."

"He does?" Bela surprised herself as she articulated her growing doubts. But Michael looked deep into her eyes, his own not flinching, as if to will her to believe like he did.

"Yes, I'm sure of it."

Chapter 2

Milana

Milana watched from the side of the large, mirrored room as her son, Alikhan, leaned against the wall and pulled his right ankle up behind him, stretching and loosening his quad muscles after the dance lesson. He was in the best shape he'd ever been in, but he couldn't afford any injuries at this point, not with the regional championships coming up. His dance ensemble, Talinka, was one of the most prestigious, and she knew that he would do anything to be able to represent them in the regionals. At just fifteen years old he wasn't quite in the same league as some of the older dancers, like Medik and Safarbi, but he had talent, and a strong sense of self-belief.

The teacher said some final words to all the students and then dismissed them. Milana detected a collective sigh of relief. It was a great honour to be in the ensemble, but having to practise five days a week for two hours at a time was taking its toll on some of the younger boys and girls. Alikhan was struggling to keep his grades up and stay on top of his homework, and he wasn't the only one. At least school was out for the summer now.

Alikhan spotted her across the room and jogged over. Just as he reached her, a familiar voice came from behind.

"Your spins are really coming along."

Milana glanced around to see a tall girl with raven black hair and dark eyes that sparkled.

Alikhan grinned at her. "I saw you'd been chosen for the front row in the third dance, well done," he replied.

"Hello, Alyona, how are you?" said Milana warmly.

"Hello. Good, thank you." The girl smiled at her but then turned her attention back to Alikhan.

Alikhan and Alyona had been friends pretty much since they were born. Milana had met Alyona's mother, Madina, when they were both out pushing their prams one day, and their friendship had flourished. They'd both felt quite lonely in the village, but for different reasons. Milana was missing the exciting life of Shekala, where she'd grown up. Madina, on the other hand, was dealing with a husband who didn't love her and who had started having affairs while she was pregnant with their baby. Alyona was a year older than Alikhan, but neither of them had siblings, so it had been natural for them to seek each other out as playmates. Milana and Madina had both encouraged it, glad to be able to spend more time together themselves. Sadly, Madina and Alyona had left the village seven years ago, after Madina's marriage finally broke down. The children had gone to different schools and not seen each other for a long time. Until, that is, when Alikhan had turned up for his first dance class at Talinka earlier this year only to find that Alyona was also a dancer here. They'd picked up their friendship again as naturally as if they'd only been away from each other for a week or two. Milana was also more than happy to renew her friendship with Madina.

"Mama mentioned something about us all going out for a *shawarma*, are you interested?" Alyona nodded in the direction of the door, where Madina was chatting to another mother.

"Sure, sounds great. I'll just grab my stuff," said Alikhan quickly. "Um, if that's okay with you, Mama?"

"Of course, sounds great," Milana answered with a smile. Going to The Orange Café after dance practice was becoming a bit of a Friday night habit for the four of them. The Orange Café, as they affectionately called it because of its bright orange décor, made the best *shawarmas* in town, and Milana's mouth was already salivating at the thought of the flour tortilla wraps with their filling of beef strips, mayonnaise and lettuce. She and Madina would have a good natter over coffee afterwards, while Alikhan and Alyona enjoyed their milkshakes.

It was an easy, ten-minute walk from the *Dom Pionerov*, where the dance rehearsals took place, to the Orange Café. The two teenagers soon strode ahead, leaving Milana and Madina able to talk without being overheard.

"How's Alikhan feeling about the regionals coming up?" asked Madina.

"Oh, you know, a bit nervous, but I think he'll be ready. How about Alyona?"

"She's so excited. You know Alyona. Everything in life is so much fun."

Milana smiled at Madina's words, her eyes resting

on their two children just ahead. "I can't believe how much they've both grown up. It seems only yesterday we were pushing our prams together," she said.

"Do you remember we used to joke about them getting married," said Madina.

They both laughed. "Yes. We pictured ourselves old and grey, doting grandmothers together."

"I guess it's still on the cards?" Madina's eyes twinkled playfully as she said this. Milana looked first at her and then back at the two figures in front of them. They certainly did seem to be getting along well. "Perhaps," she replied, "But it's a bit early yet, isn't it?"

"Oh, I don't know," said Madina. "Lots of Alyona's school friends seem to be pairing off already."

"But, I'm not ready for that yet!" protested Milana. "Can't we just keep them young forever?"

There was a moment of silence, and Milana sensed a shift in Madina's thinking. "Are you alright? Alikhan's a good catch, any girl would be lucky to have him," she said, hoping to get a smile out of her friend.

"No, no, it's not that," said Madina, still thoughtful.

"What is it then?"

"It's Musa."

"Your ex?" Oh dear, this couldn't be good. It had taken Madina so long to disentangle herself from that good-for-nothing, cheating husband of hers and finally get back on her feet again.

"Yes. He called me the other day. It was a bit of a shock, actually."

"What did he want?"

Madina took in a deep breath. "He said he was sorry he had been an absent father and that he wanted to see more of Alyona."

"Oh." From what Milana could remember, her

friend's ex hadn't shown any interest in his daughter since the day she was born and he'd found out that she was a girl and not the son that he was expecting. "What did you say?"

"I said I'd think about it. And talk it over with Alyona, of course."

Milana looked at the carefree, smiling girl waiting for them by the entrance to the café. "How do you think she'll take it?"

Madina sighed. "I honestly don't know. She blames her father for the divorce, of course. I tried not to turn her against him, but, well, the facts speak for themselves really. That, and the small matter that he hasn't made any attempt to contact her in the whole of the last seven years."

Milana gave her friend's hand a quick squeeze. "Let me know what you decide. And call me if you need a chat, okay?"

"Okay, thanks."

They reached the café entrance and all four of them went in to find their usual table.

Later that evening, after Alikhan had gone to bed, Milana sat in the family living room watching television with her husband, Murat, and her in-laws. She couldn't help thinking about Madina's situation. What would she do in her place? She looked across at Murat, sitting comfortably next to his mother on the sofa. He was a good man, her Murat. She'd never had any reason to doubt his faithfulness to her. There had never been any hint of other women or roving eyes. Her in-laws were good people too. They had always treated her kindly, unlike Madina's mother-in-law who had treated her more like a housemaid.

Yet, as she mulled over her friend's dilemma, she

couldn't help but feel a pang of concern deep within her chest. All the people in this room shared a secret that Alikhan was blissfully unaware of. They each knew something that he didn't, and that was that he too had an absent father. In fact, one he'd never laid eyes on, not even as a baby. What would happen if Alikhan's real father suddenly showed up on the scene asking to see him? No, that couldn't happen. She'd been more than clear when they broke up that there would be no contact whatsoever. It was best for the baby, she'd said. He'd seemed convinced, and that was an end to it. They'd all moved on. Alikhan was happy. Murat was a wonderful father. No, nothing would happen to rock Alikhan's world the way Alyona's was about to be rocked, she would make sure of that.

Chapter 3

Azamat

Azamat turned off the lights and closed the door to the shop behind him, turning the key in the lock. He gave a final look through the shop window just to check that everything was in order, and then jogged down the steps and onto the pavement below. Sometimes he still had to remind himself that this wasn't all a dream. Who'd have thought that he, lazy, drop-out, good-for-nothing Azamat, would actually own his own business and be doing fairly well at it too? Okay, so he still had a large loan to pay back, but the American, Cody Eriksson, was generous and fair. Azamat had first met him just over seven years ago lifting weights at the gym here in Shekala. The American had moved down to the Caucasus to start a tourism business, and he had one of those magnetic personalities that instantly drew you to him. He had a big heart and a warm smile, but you knew also that he was sharp, and you wouldn't get away with trying to take advantage of the fact that he was a Westerner.

Ignoring his old Lada parked just a few feet away,

Azamat crossed over the road at the end of the block and kept on walking, his stride confident and purposeful. He was enjoying the slightly cooler, fresher air on this July evening and felt like stretching his legs. It had been another long day of sweltering in a shop with just a couple of fans for air conditioning. He would walk right to the end of Oktyabraskaya Street and back.

Many people were milling around on the streets, making their way home from work or from the market. Others, mostly students, were on their way out for the evening. The university wasn't too far away, and small clusters of young people hung around on corners and near the entrance to bars. Azamat paid them no attention. His mind was elsewhere, thinking back to the events that had got him where he was today. He'd grown up tinkering with cars in the village, no real thought of a career. After his army duty, at nineteen, he'd got caught up with a terrorist organisation, and had only just been able to pull himself away in time. He shuddered to think what would have happened if he hadn't seen sense and come back home. He'd probably be dead by now.

Cody, and his British room-mate Michael, had taken him under their wing. Michael had employed him as a language helper, and just that one act, the offer of a steady job and some income, albeit just a couple of hours a week, had been the start of Azamat's life turning around.

It had been Cody's idea to open the bike shop. He'd wanted it as part of his tourism service, encouraging cyclists to come and enjoy the breath-taking views of the Caucasus mountain range.

Most tourists would come and hire a bike for a day, and ride around the large town park, stopping for a meal in the cafés by the man-made lake at the top. Other, more serious cyclists would bring their own bikes, but they needed somewhere to go for repairs and to get advice about the best long-distance routes. Business had definitely been slower over the winter, and he had used the out-of-season time to learn more about different bike models and how to order the spare parts that might be needed. But now, the season was in full flow, and each day was busy and interesting. There was the bike race to look forward to as well; he couldn't wait to talk more about that with Cody.

As he approached the corner of Oktyabraskaya Street, Azamat hesitated and looked down towards the large grey apartment blocks next to the row of shops. Perhaps he had time to stop by his sister's house? He wasn't due to meet his father for another couple of hours, but maybe he could just hang around here in town for a bit longer. There was no need to go all the way back to his home village of Awush just for a few hours. Besides, he hadn't seen Bela for a month or so. It would be good to see Michael too. Azamat grinned. Bela and Michael getting together was in some part thanks to him. He'd been the one to introduce them at that party after all.

He strode up to the apartment block and tapped in the code on the door. He ran up the three flights of steps, taking them two at a time. He needed to keep in shape. Sitting in a shop day in day out was beginning to take its toll on his physique. He missed the physical drills of the army. It had been tough, but he'd revelled in the chance to push his endurance to the limits and see his body getting stronger and leaner each day. These days it was up to him to try to work some exercise into his daily routine.

He reached Bela's apartment and rang the doorbell.

"Azamat! This is a welcome surprise." Bela stood there in a pale green summer dress, her long black hair tied up in a loose bun behind her head.

Azamat grinned and showed her his empty hands. "Sorry, little sis, no gift. This was a bit of a spur of the moment decision. Just wanted to check how you were all doing."

"Of course, come in. Michael will be home in half an hour."

"Actually, that would be great. I'm supposed to be meeting Papa in town this evening, but you know he always works later than he says. I'm expecting a text any minute telling me he's running late again."

Bela laughed. "Yep, sounds like Papa." She disappeared into the kitchen.

Azamat carefully removed his shoes and walked into the living room. Sure enough, Angelina was in there watching television. She turned when she saw him and gave him a big grin.

"Uncle Azamat!"

"Hey, there, pumpkin." Azamat tousled her head affectionately. Angelina was a sweet girl. She reminded him so much of her mother, Zalina, who had grown up next door to them in the village and who had been in Azamat's year at school.

Bela appeared with a glass of water. "Here you go. It's so hot again today!"

"Thanks. Yeah, I've already spoken to Cody about installing proper air conditioning in the shop. It's like an oven in there. I'm sure it's not good for business."

"I'll put a good word in for you tomorrow," Bela said. As Cody's personal assistant, she had quite a bit of sway when it came to practical arrangements.

Azamat settled himself into one of the sofa chairs, half an eye on the television show that Angelina was watching. "He's treating you well, this English husband of yours?" he asked Bela.

Bela laughed. "Yes, of course, he's a wonderful husband."

"Just had to ask. Big brotherly concern and all that."

"What about you, how are things?" Bela perched on the arm of the sofa chair just across from him.

"Great. Busy. Cody and I are just putting finishing touches to the plans for the bike race at the end of August. That should attract a few more experienced cyclists, and who knows, it might just become an annual thing."

"I know, he talks about nothing else at the moment. Looks like several well-known names in the cycling world have signed up already. How are things at home?"

"Oh, you know, the same. Mama's still busy around the house, always fussing. Papa's still working long hours."

"Uncle Artur?" Bela had always had a soft spot for their wayward Uncle, who'd become a serious alcoholic over the years, after first losing his wife and son and then losing his job in the economic crisis in the early nineties.

"The same."

"And you, Azamat?" Bela lowered her voice. "Have you had any news of ..." She glanced across at Angelina and then mouthed the words "your son?"

Azamat felt a pang in his chest. A few years ago, he'd told Bela the whole story of how he'd got his girlfriend pregnant when he was eighteen, and how she'd kept the baby but got married to someone else and forbidden him to have any contact. He gave a deep sigh and hung his head. Perhaps he shouldn't have told anyone. Just kept the secret to himself. But then it had felt so good to share his pain with someone else. He trusted Bela not to tell anyone, but it felt uncomfortable when she pressed him for information.

He glanced over at Angelina, who genuinely seemed to be totally engrossed in her cartoon. He looked back at Bela and kept his voice low.

"No. I keep trying to build up courage to go to the village where they live and try to catch a glimpse, but I just can't seem to do it."

Bela reached over and gave his hand a sympathetic squeeze. "Maybe the time's not right, yet. Maybe one day."

"Yes, maybe one day."

Azamat turned his eyes back to the television, but he couldn't focus. His son. Why could he still not let it go, even after all these years? Why did it still hurt to think about it?

There was a fumbling sound of a key in the lock and the creak of the front door opening. Bela jumped up from the arm rest where she'd been perching, a big smile on her face. Michael was home.

"We're in here. Azamat's come for a visit." She switched from speaking Circassian, their native tongue, to speaking Russian. Michael's Circassian was still a little shaky, but his Russian was excellent. Azamat also switched easily to Russian.

"Hey, Michael. How are things?" He gave Michael a handshake and a friendly slap on the back.

"Great, thanks. It's good to see you, Azamat. How are things with you?"

"Also great. Just checking up on my little sister here."

The two men moved through to the kitchen, where Bela presented them both with a plate of fried chicken, macaroni and a bowl of cucumber and tomato salad mixed with *smetana* and dill. Azamat was about to start eating, when he remembered that Michael and Bela liked to pray before they ate. He stopped himself just in time and bowed his head with the others.

"Thank you, Lord, for all your good gifts to us. Thank you for this food and for bringing our guest Azamat to us today. We ask your blessing on him and on our conversation together. Amen."

"Amen," mumbled Azamat. It was getting less uncomfortable listening to his sister and her husband praying like that, but it did still seem a little weird. He put a forkful of macaroni in his mouth. Bela went to call Angelina in for dinner now that the men were served.

"Your job at the bike shop is going well?" Michael asked

"Yes, I love it. I actually look forward to going to work every day. I know there's not a lot of people who can say that about their jobs," Azamat replied.

Michael looked thoughtfully at him. "You know, it's so great to see you smiling and happy. You've changed so much in the last couple of years."

Azamat laughed. "Yes, I'm a changed man. I have a steady job and great plans for my business. Things couldn't be better."

"On the outside everything looks great. I'm proud of you," said Michael. "But is everything truly changed on the inside?"

Azamat furrowed his brows. How much did Michael know about his past? They'd talked before about Azamat's involvement in the terrorist group, but had Bela told him more?

"I, er. I still have some things I'm dealing with, I guess." He tried to laugh it off, but Michael wasn't fooled.

"Don't leave it too late to forgive yourself for your past mistakes, Azamat. Forgive and let go."

Azamat opened his mouth but then shut it again. What did Michael mean? What did forgiveness have to do with anything?

At that moment Angelina scampered in, with Bela not far behind. He'd have to continue his talk with Michael another time.

It was late when he finally left Bela and Michael's apartment. The rest of the evening had been full of light banter, nothing serious. But as Azamat headed out onto the street, he just couldn't get his head straight. He was nervous, that's what it was. He'd asked Papa to meet up with him after work tonight to talk through a business proposition. He and Cody had been fleshing out the details of the upcoming summer bike race, but it needed approval from the local government, and Azamat was hoping that Papa might be able to put in a good word for them with his colleagues. He was well-prepared. He had a print-out of projected income for local businesses as a result of the extra tourism that the race would generate, as well as a detailed plan of the suggested route, necessary road closures and the number of people they would need to hire as marshals at the various intersections. There was even a list of potential sponsors for the event, who were hoping to gain back what they were putting in through advertising along the race route. It was a solid proposition. So why was his heart pounding more quickly than usual, and why were his hands so sweaty? Was it because of what Michael had said, or was it something else?

He glanced at the clock. Papa had texted as expected, and they'd arranged to meet just after ten o'clock. It was already dark outside. It had been his idea to meet Papa in town, in a neutral place, rather than at home. He'd wanted to make this a serious meeting, one businessman to another. At home he always felt like he was sixteen again and that his father disapproved of everything he did. As the only son, it was his duty to stay at the family home to look after his parents, but until he was married himself, he'd always be treated like a schoolboy. Although he didn't mind it when Mama spoiled him. He'd always be her little boy. Her only son. She'd been so worried when he'd dropped out of contact for a year or two after the army, and he'd promised her that he'd never do that again.

However, if he had gone home first rather than lingering at Bela and Michael's, then maybe his head would be clearer. Certain conversations at their place had forced his mind to start dwelling on the past once more. Images flitted in and out from his memory as he walked along, most of them unbidden and unwanted. Images of his time in training with the terrorist organisation up near Moscow. Television images of the aftermath of the Beslan tragedy, that haunted him still, every night, nearly six years later. He could have been there. He could have been one of the ones responsible. Sometimes in his dreams he saw himself as a parent, standing outside the school, helpless, knowing his own son was in there. He would wake up, drenched in sweat, crying out his son's name. But his son hadn't been there, thank God. Zalina's son, had, though. She, her son and her husband. What if he'd been directly responsible for their deaths? He'd grown up next door to Zalina. They'd been the same age.

Azamat shuddered and picked up the pace a little. He thought about his son. In his dreams he could never properly make out his son's face. He'd never laid eyes on him in real life. He'd be fifteen years old now. Had Milana ever told him the truth? Did he know that the man he thought was his father wasn't his real father? He'd asked himself so many times if he should try to get in contact, but each time he kept remembering the stern look on Milana's face.

"Please don't come looking for the baby, will you? Please don't cause trouble. If you ever loved me, you'll leave me alone. Okay?". Was she right? Was it really better that his son never knew the truth? And what about *his* rights? Did she ever consider his feelings, that he might actually want to see his own son one day?

He and his father weren't meeting for another fifteen minutes, but something inside him suddenly caused him to tense up. Adrenaline pulsed through his veins. Not the same kind of edgy nervousness he'd been feeling these last few minutes about meeting up with his father. No, this was different. Something in his gut told him that he needed to hurry. He needed to go and meet his father right now. It was as if he was being compelled by an invisible force outside of himself. He clutched his folder of papers tighter to his chest and rounded the corner where the bar was located. Something wasn't right. He needed to move faster. He broke into a jog. He reached the place where they had agreed to meet, but the invisible force wouldn't let him stop. He needed to keep going. His heart was beating really fast now. What was going on?

Azamat turned another corner and entered the town park. A soft glow from the lampposts lighted up the path before him. He jogged down towards the middle and then took a right, towards the part of the park nearest to the building where his father worked. The light was dimmer here. Some of the lamps were no longer working. Up ahead, in the distance, he could just make out a figure walking towards him. He slowed down, relieved. It looked like his father, his bulky frame striding purposefully, a briefcase swinging in his hand. But there was someone else, behind him. Someone in the shadows.

Whoever it was caught up with his father. Azamat couldn't see what was happening, but they were talking. Azamat kept walking towards his father, straining to see in the darkness. Something was very wrong. The other man grabbed Papa by the arm and Papa dropped his suitcase.

"Hey!" Azamat shouted. He started sprinting towards his father. The stranger looked up and Azamat caught a brief glimpse of his face. A young man, he couldn't have been more than about nineteen or twenty. He looked angry. He turned back towards Papa and suddenly a shot rang out. Azamat knew that sound. He hadn't gone through all that training in the army not to recognise the sound of a Glock 17. He reached his father a second later. His father collapsed to the ground, clutching his stomach. Azamat looked up at the young man who was sprinting off into the darkness of the park beyond. For a split second he thought about chasing him. Anger coursed through his entire body. How dare he shoot his father; he would pay for what he'd done! But he knew if he chased him then he would have to leave his father all alone. With all the strength of mind he could summon up he turned his attention back to his father and let the young man go.

Chapter 4

Bela

Bela, Mama and Madina pushed their way through the crowd of people at the entrance to the hospital. They hastily pulled on the obligatory white hospital coats over their own clothes, and wrapped the blue, plastic shoe covers over their sandals.

"Where is he?" Mama asked, her voice high-pitched and trembling, and her eyes displaying a fear that Bela had rarely seen before.

Madina took her hand. "Don't worry, Mama, I'm sure everything will be alright. Azamat said he was on the sixth floor."

Bela exchanged a worried glance with her older sister. Would everything really be alright? It wasn't every day that your father got shot. She still couldn't believe it. Azamat had phoned them late last night, but they hadn't been able to get into the hospital until this morning. Mama was already striding towards the staircase, and Bela and Madina hurried after her, carrying their bag of supplies. They hadn't known what to bring, hadn't known

41

what kind of situation their father would be in, so in the end they'd just settled on some blankets and cushions to make the hospital bed more comfortable.

A few minutes later the three women arrived, panting a little, at the top of the staircase on the sixth floor. Azamat was in the long, bare corridor, squatting down against the white-washed wall. He sprang up when he saw them and gave Mama a hug and a kiss. His eyes were bloodshot with dark rings, the result of a long, sleepless night in an uncomfortable position. Chairs for visitors to sit on were few and far between in this hospital.

"They've finished operating, Mama. They think he's going to be okay, but they're just making sure."

"Oh, thank God!" Mama swooned and might have fallen to the floor if Bela and Madina hadn't been right behind her.

"Can we see him?" Bela asked.

"I don't know. I'll tell the doctors you're here."

After half an hour of anxious waiting, the door opened, and they were finally ushered into her father's room. Bela hadn't been prepared for the shock of seeing her proud, determined, authoritative father lying so weak and helpless in a hospital bed. His face was pale and drawn, his eyes closed. Tubes ran out from underneath the bedclothes and attached themselves to various pieces of hospital equipment.

Mama ran to the bed and clutched her husband's hand in hers.

"Aslan! Aslan, can you hear me?"

Papa turned his head slowly towards her and opened his eyes. Everyone breathed a sigh of relief. Bela left Mama and Madina to fuss over her father while she went back towards the door to join Azamat, who was in deep conversation with the doctor.

"The next few days are obviously critical, but we're fairly confident at this point. Miraculously, the bullet didn't damage any major organs, but he did lose a lot of blood."

"What can we do? What does he need?" Bela asked.

The doctor turned to her, his haughty eyes pretending to be concerned and sympathetic. No doubt he knew who his patient was. "We will make sure Aslan Kadirovich has every comfort, and I expect him to be transferred to a private room soon. I will give you a list of medicines you need to buy. He will be too weak to eat anything today, but you might like to bring some soup tomorrow."

"Yes, yes of course." Bela turned her eyes back to her father.

The doctor cleared his throat. "There will, of course, be an inquiry. The police will be asking questions."

Azamat looked stern. "We hope they find the monster that did this as soon as possible and that he gets locked up for life."

Bela studied her brother. It had been a long time since she'd seen him so strong, so determined, so much in control. It was good but it also unnerved her. He had witnessed the shooting, after all. In their culture that was enough for someone to take the law into their own hands and seek revenge the old-fashioned way. A blood feud between two families that could last generations.

Please God, don't let that happen.

Three days later Papa's condition was much improved, according to the doctors, and he was now able to sit up and eat the soup that Mama spoon-fed him. Mama had spent each night sleeping in a chair in Papa's hospital room, and Bela had had to force her to go home for a bit to rest.

"Okay, okay, I'll just go and wash and change into some clean clothes," Mama had agreed reluctantly. "You'll be here the whole time?"

"Yes, Mama, don't worry. Go, and maybe lie down on a proper bed for an hour or two. You need to keep your strength up."

Papa was still sleeping, so Bela settled herself down in the chair and took out the book she'd brought with her. She looked at the cover, admiring the glossy photo on the front. It was Michael who was getting her to read books; she hadn't really read much before. Ever since he'd introduced her to the Christian bookshop run by their church, she couldn't seem to get enough, and had been devouring a book a week. This particular book was written by an American and translated into Russian. Someone called Yancey, and something about grace. She was learning such a lot about her new faith, but the more she read the more she realised she had to learn and the more questions she had. She sighed. She'd never catch up to where Michael was. There were so many new concepts to learn, and so many old beliefs to expose and replace. She realised how wrong she'd been about God for so many years.

Papa stirred, muttered something, but sank back into a deep sleep again. The door opened and Azamat came in. He looked at Papa and slowed his steps, not wanting to disturb him, but there was something in his eyes that made Bela's heart start to race. She jumped up and followed Azamat into the corridor, where they could talk more openly.

"What is it? Is there news?"

"Yes. They've caught him!" Azamat looked jubilant.

"How? Where?"

"He was trying to board an overnight bus to Moscow, and he fit the description I gave the police, so the driver kept him talking until the police arrived. He's being held in the main police station here in Shekala, and they're questioning him right now."

Bela was stunned and a little shaken. She'd been so focussed on her father's recovery that she hadn't given much thought to the motive behind the shooting.

"Do they know why he did it?"

"No, not yet, but it looks like he was acting alone."

"How do you know all this?"

Azamat smiled slyly. "Let's just say, I have friends in high places."

Bela didn't press him further. Either he knew someone who shouldn't have been telling him so much, or he'd been passing money under the table. Either way, she didn't want to know.

"Is there anything else?"

Azamat laughed. "Just that the idiot is claiming that Papa is his father. Can you believe that! People will say anything to get themselves off the hook. I mean, how ridiculous!"

Bela felt the blood drain from her cheeks. She stumbled back towards the wall, her mind whirring.

"You said, before, that he was a young man. About twenty-one?"

"Yes, perhaps. I would have put him younger, maybe about nineteen. What? What is it?"

"And he was boarding a bus to Moscow?"

"Yes. What is it Bela? You're scaring me now. Do you know something I don't know?"

"Oh, Azamat. Is his name Pavlik? That is, I guess he'd be going by his full name, Pavel, now."

Now it was Azamat's turn to go pale. He stared at Bela in disbelief. "Yes," he said quietly. "He gave his name as Pavel Aslanovich Shatinov. How would you know that?"

Bela looked at her brother and sighed. "I think it's time I told you something. A secret I've been keeping quiet for too long."

Chapter 5

Bela

By the end of the week, Papa was doing much better and would be released into Mama's care at home in a few days' time. Bela couldn't stop thinking about Pavel and what he'd done. What he'd tried to do.

Lord, what would drive him to try to kill Papa, a man he'd never really met? What was he trying to gain? I don't understand.

Her thoughts swirled round in her mind no matter how much she prayed about it. At least it was keeping her mind off the whole pregnancy thing, or rather the lack of pregnancy. She broached the subject of Pavel again with Michael that evening, when Angelina was tucked up in bed and they were sitting together, just the two of them, on the sofa in their living room.

"I just feel like I should do something."

"But what? What can you do?" Michael was always so logical about everything. "Pavel's in custody and the police are waiting for your father to press charges."

"He's taking his time about it. When he found out who it was who'd shot him, he went all funny. You should have seen his face. It was like he'd seen a ghost."

"Surely they'll convict Pavel anyway, whether your father presses charges or not? He did try to kill a man."

"Yes, but my father has a lot of power in the local government. He could get Pavel's case dropped just like that if he wanted to."

"You think he's hesitating because it's his son?"

"Yes, of course. Family is everything here, even estranged, deranged sons who try to kill you. Maybe Papa's feeling guilty about cutting Pavel out of his life. Do you think that's why Pavel tried to kill him?"

"What, because your father cut him out of his life? I guess it's possible. He sent money though, didn't he?"

"I don't know. I know he sent a little, back when I was in Moscow in 1999, because I was the one who had to hand deliver the envelopes."

Bela paused. A memory sprang to mind. That time when Pavel's mother, Maria, had confronted her in the entrance hall of the apartment building and told her about Pavel's illness. The extra money that Papa had sent for the hospital bills had ruined Bela's chances of going to England and effectively ended her university education too.

Michael stroked her hair and kissed her on the cheek. "I think it's late and you need to get some sleep."

"I'm going to visit him!" Bela blurted out, suddenly. "I'm going to visit Pavel in the police station."

"Are you sure that's wise?" A frown of concern fell over Michael's face, but somehow it only made Bela feel more determined.

"I just have to know what drove him to it. I have to know more about his past. He is my half-brother after all."

Bela's hands fidgeted under the table while she waited for the guard to bring Pavel to talk to her. She glanced at Michael, who had insisted on coming with her. He seemed on edge too. Was she making a mistake coming here? She hadn't seen her half-brother since he was about three. It had been the first time she'd found out that Papa had a mistress; that he was being unfaithful to Mama. Maria, Pavel's mother, had turned up at their home in the village and demanded money from Papa. He'd driven them away quickly, but Bela had overheard the conversation and had seen the terrified little boy clutching his mother's legs. The woman had looked very different when they'd met in Moscow eight years later. If Papa had been sending them money, he hadn't been sending very much.

The door opened and a guard walked in, followed by a thin youth with unkempt, unwashed hair. His eyes betrayed both nervousness and defiance at the same time. There was no mistaking he was related; it was like looking at a younger version of her brother Azamat.

Bela stood up but then sat down again. What was the proper etiquette when you were visiting potential prisoners? She probably shouldn't shake his hand, so she placed hers on the table. The guard motioned Pavel to sit down in the chair opposite and then stood at a slight distance.

"Who are you?" growled Pavel, looking first at Bela and then at Michael.

"I'm Bela. I'm your…" She glanced at the guard. Did they know that Pavel was her father's son? Pavel had claimed he was, but had her father confirmed it? Or was she about to give away a family secret? She hadn't really thought this through.

"I'm Aslan Kadirovich's daughter," she said eventually. "You shot my father."

Pavel's eyes widened as he took in this news. He looked at her with a new interest, obviously realising now that she was his half-sister. How much did he know about his other family? His eyes darkened and his gruff demeanour returned.

"Why are you here?"

"I… I just wanted to know why. Why did you do it?"

Pavel rolled his eyes and slumped back in his chair, his arms folded. "That man ruined my mother's life. He ruined my life."

"How? How did he ruin your life?"

Pavel straightened up and leaned forward. He looked Bela in the eyes, perhaps trying to work out how much she knew about the situation. Bela instinctively sat back a little. He scared her, but she didn't want him to know that.

"Because of him my mother and I grew up in poverty," he growled. "She never managed to pull her life together. She… we…struggled to get enough food, while *your father*," he sneered as he said those words, "was living the high life down here."

"But it wasn't like that!" Bela glanced at the guard again and checked herself. "I'm… sure it wasn't like that."

"How would you know?" Pavel looked at her with such hatred that Bela shuffled backwards in her chair. She was suddenly glad the guard was there. Michael grabbed her hand and held it tightly. What might Pavel have done if she'd been alone? Would he have tried to hurt her too? Did he think that she was part of some big conspiracy to ruin his life?

"We're done here," said Pavel suddenly. He got up and indicated to the guard to open the door back towards his cell. Bela was going to object but stopped herself. There was no way they were going to have a proper conversation here with the guard listening. How could she defend herself and defend Papa without betraying Papa's secret? She stood up and let the guard escort Pavel away. When they'd left she noticed both her hands were trembling. She clung tightly onto Michael's arm to steady herself as they walked out of the building. What a relief to be back outside on the street again, safe.

Chapter 6

Azamat

Azamat listened to Bela's story of visiting Pavel in police custody, the muscles in his jaw and fists tightening. How could she have done such a stupid thing? That guy was a dangerous lunatic. What was Michael thinking, letting his wife do that, even if he was there with her? Didn't he care about Bela?

Of course he did. Azamat took a deep breath. He would try to hear Bela's side of the story before he did anything rash. He'd learned that, at least, over the years; that it didn't pay to be hasty and act in anger.

"But, Azamat, he's our brother. I just felt I had to see him."

"*Half*-brother. Apparently." He still couldn't believe the story that Bela had told him, about Papa having a secret mistress and child all those years ago.

"I kind of believe him, though. I saw his mother, remember, all those years ago. She looked haggard and awful. She was desperate for money."

"Of course she was. She was probably spending it

on drugs." Why did Bela have to always see the best in people? She was so naïve.

"But even if she was, what drove her to that? What would it have been like for Pavel to grow up in that kind of environment?"

"So, you're saying he tried to kill Papa because Papa hadn't given him enough money?" Azamat was struggling to keep his temper at bay. How could Bela be defending this idiot, this madman?

"Something like that."

"And you believe him?"

"I don't know what to believe. What makes a young man want to kill his own father? Especially a father he doesn't even know?"

Later that evening, as he lay on his bed, Azamat couldn't get Bela's words out of his head. What did make a young man so angry at a father he never knew? A chill ran through his body, and he sat up, his heart thumping loudly inside his chest. What if his own son was already incubating this kind of anger inside him? Was his own situation any different? He had walked away from his own son because Milana had told him to, but what kind of repercussions would that have later down the line? Would his own son seek him out and try to kill him too?

He shook his head and stood up. He was being stupid. His son, Alikhan, if that really was his name, was being brought up in a respectable, well-off family. Milana had assured him of that. Her words echoed in his mind. *"It's for the best, Azamat. It's best for the baby too. It will be well looked after. It'll have a stable life."*

But even so, did he really want his son hating him? What had Milana told Alikhan about him? Would he know how much Azamat had longed to see him over the years, how painful it had been to keep his distance, how he had wanted to be that baby's father right from the start? Who would tell him that?

He felt such an ache in his chest it was like his heart was breaking. Come on, it had been fifteen years. Why was it still so painful to think about? Was the father-son bond really that strong? Oh, he'd been so stupid just to walk away. He should have stayed. He should have insisted on having a part in Alikhan's life. He'd been weak and too easily swayed by Milana's arguments. Walking away had seemed like the brave thing to do at the time, but now he could see that it had actually been the cowardly option.

Argh! Azamat hit his fist on the table. Just when his life was turning around. Just when he'd started feeling truly happy. Why now?

The conversation with Michael just before his father's shooting replayed in his mind. Forgive himself, Michael had suggested. Azamat had assumed Michael was talking about Beslan, but maybe he was talking about more than that.

Azamat sat back down on his bed and held his head in his hands. He'd done some stupid things when he was younger - stealing, breaking into a car, messing around with drink and drugs. But it was when he walked away from Milana and his unborn child that things had really spiralled downhill. Was that why he'd been drafted so easily into the terrorist organisation? Because he hadn't had the guts to face his own failure as a parent? Because he hadn't forgiven himself for walking away? He'd just buried the past deep inside, not wanting to deal with it. Not wanting to face his demons. Perhaps he'd been wrong. He needed to ask Michael more about this forgiveness thing.

Azamat gritted his jaw. But that still didn't change the present situation. He'd walked away from his son fifteen years ago, just like his own father had, and history was on its way to repeating itself. He needed to find his son before it was too late. He had to. There was no way he was going to repeat the mistakes his father had made. There was no way he was going to end up with a son who hated him so much he wished him dead. Besides, he had a right to be part of Alikhan's life, didn't he? He'd let Milana push him away, but no longer. He just had to figure out a way to slot himself back into his son's life, and that wasn't going to be easy.

Chapter 7

Milana

It was the day of the regionals. The dance ensemble had had their final rehearsal the previous day, and Alikhan had come home sweaty and exhausted. Milana had done her best to encourage him, but secretly she was glad that the pressure would soon be coming to an end. It was the middle of September, but the weather was still stiflingly hot outside, and the ensemble director seemed to have no pity. If he wanted them fresh and rested for the big day, then he would have let them go home sooner.

Milana settled in her seat next to Madina and turned her attention to the stage. Behind the curtain the young people would be stretching and practising their dance steps one last time. The girls would be fixing their tall hats on their heads and arranging their long, white veils so they flowed down their backs, covering their long plaits. She felt a yearning to be part of that again. Being able to move gracefully around the dance floor, her feet hidden under her long dress so that it looked like she was floating on air. Delicately moving her hands in and out, out and in. Now spinning, now swapping sides. Demure and delicate but also strong and proud. She had loved dancing, why had she given it up? She'd preferred spending time hanging out with her friends in the park. Hanging out with Alikhan's father.

The musicians suddenly sprang into action.

"They're starting," whispered Madina. She seemed equally excited.

Milana watched the accordion player sweeping the sides of the traditional instrument in and out, out and in. The drums beat time to the music and beat deep into her soul also.

The first two group dances went perfectly. Soon it was time for the boys to show what they could do. Milana recognised one of Alikhan's friends, Medik. He leaped high into the air, arching his back so that his toes almost touched his head, and then landed on his knees before leaping up again. She winced as he hit the floor. She knew how much it hurt, though Medik didn't show it. Each boy was proud to be a member of Talinka. Proud to be Circassian. Proud of their culture, their heritage. They were brave; they were warriors.

Now it was Alikhan's turn. Milana held her breath as she watched her son spin around the room on his knees, perfectly in time to the music, perfectly in control. He reached the end and leaped up to a round of applause, bowing proudly, his head held high and his arms lifted up, elbows out, one fist to his chest, the other arm now straight. She felt sure she must be the proudest parent in the room, as she clapped fiercely, almost rising out of her seat, but the dance was continuing and she would have to wait till the end.

Madina had applauded Alikhan loudly too, but her attention would be on her own daughter. Milana's eyes scoured the stage seeking out Alyona and found her near the front of the group of girls on the right. She had grown into a real beauty, that girl. She couldn't believe she was sixteen already, and her own son already fifteen. The two women shared a smile and then focussed back on the dancers. They'd done really well, the Talinka ensemble. Surely, they were in with a chance of winning the whole thing.

Madina leant over and whispered, "Seems like only yesterday they were both in prams, doesn't it?"

Milana smiled and nodded. There were two more dance ensembles to go. This current group was good, but not as good as Alikhan's, she was sure of it. She allowed her thoughts to wander, her interest no longer held by the performers on the stage. Her son was such an amazing dancer, so talented. He got that from her, obviously. Murat, on the other hand, seemed to have two left feet. Alikhan certainly didn't get it from him. But then… She caught herself. Of course, he wouldn't, would he? He didn't get anything from Murat, really. Murat wasn't Alikhan's real father.

Milana didn't often allow herself to think of Alikhan's real father, but she couldn't help it, here, watching the dancing. After all, it had been in a dance group just like this that she'd first met Azamat.

Azamat.

She didn't allow herself to think that name.

Azamat.

Something inside of her tightened. Was it guilt stabbing her heart again? Azamat should be here, clapping his son, being proud of him too. But he wasn't, and that was all her doing. She'd made him promise to stay away, to never see his child or try to contact him.

How many times in the years gone by had she wondered if she'd done the right thing? Did Alikhan have a right to know who his real father was? Should she tell him? No, that would be silly. They hadn't seen each other in years. He'd probably moved on. Maybe he was married with his own children by now. She pushed her thoughts down and focussed her attention back on the stage. They would be announcing the winner soon.

2

The mountains will be overturned,

the cliffs will crumble and

every wall will fall to the ground.

Ezekiel 38:20

Chapter 8

Bela

"Are you okay, honey?" Michael's concerned voice floated through the door of the bathroom from the hallway outside. "You've been in there quite a while."

"Have I? Sorry, just daydreaming." Bela quickly flushed the toilet. She watched the water swirl down the drain and made sure all trace of the red blood had swirled down with it. Another month. Another disappointment. She'd felt different this month. She could have sworn she'd had a bit of nausea, could have sworn there was a slight swelling in her belly. Her period had been two days late, and she'd even considered going to get a pregnancy test from the *apteka*. She'd allowed herself to start hoping, but now all her hopes had come crashing down. Again.

Why, God, why? Why are you doing this to us? I don't understand. I thought you were kind and loving and good, but now I'm beginning to think you're cruel and malicious and that you don't care.

She choked back a sob. Michael would be

hovering around somewhere, and she didn't want him to know how upset she was; how this trial was affecting her faith. His faith was so strong, she didn't want to rock his boat too. She took a deep breath and opened the door.

"Hey?" Michael was still there.

"Hey." She focussed her eyes down on the mottled piece of carpet that ran the length of the hallway. "Not pregnant."

"Oh, sweetie, I'm so sorry." He enveloped her in a deep hug. She appreciated his effort, but right now she just wanted to be by herself. She stood there for a few seconds, tense and rigid in his strong arms, and then pushed herself away.

"I just need a minute," she mumbled, making for the small bathroom next door where there was a bit more space to breathe than in the narrow, cramped toilet room. She was beginning to feel trapped in her own home. It had seemed so beautiful at first, but now it seemed small, dark and shabby. All those girls who thought that marrying a foreigner was the answer to their money worries!

She'd been daydreaming again, staring at the bathroom mirror, lost in thought. She must have been in there at least ten minutes. She looked at her face in the mirror one more time and forced her lips into a smile. She had to be strong for Michael and Angelina's sake. If she had to endure this trial, then so be it. She steeled herself, took a deep breath, and walked back into her normal, usual, familiar life. She found Michael in the kitchen checking email on his laptop. His forehead was furrowed as he stared at the screen. She went over and smoothed her fingers across his forehead. "You'll get wrinkles if you're not careful."

"What's that? Oh, yeah. That's the least of my worries."

Bela sat down in the chair beside him. "Money running out?" she guessed.

"Yeah, something like that. I don't think I can carry on just doing research after this year. I'm going to have to find some other source of income. It's been great while it lasted, but I can't be a student for ever."

"I think," Bela drew her mouth into a sympathetic smile, "that we both need to get away for a bit. Have a break."

Michael closed his computer lid and looked at her.

"You know, I've been thinking the same thing. Where shall we go? The mountains?"

"Well, actually, I was thinking Moscow."

"Moscow? Hardly a restful place!"

"Hey, come on," Bela teased. "You've only been there once, and I could show you around a bit. There's lots of great sights to see. You've lived in Russia for nearly three years now and you've never actually been inside the Kremlin, or been to the Bolshoi ballet, or..."

Michael laughed and kissed her. "Okay, you've won me over. Let's do it."

"Great!" Finally, something to look forward to, something else to do other than sitting around this dreary apartment waiting for a pregnancy that was never going to happen.

"Would we take Angelina with us?" Michael asked.

"No, we couldn't take her out of school. She can stay with Mama for a few days, it won't be a problem."

"So, it'll just be the two of us?" He drew her onto his lap and showered her neck with kisses. Bela laughed and pushed him away. "I'll sort out the details as soon as I can!"

Mama was looking tired. The stress of all that had happened this summer had clearly been weighing her down. Or was there more to it?

Bela brought the two glasses of compote out into the garden and handed one to Mama.

"Let's enjoy the end of the summer before it gets too cold to sit outside anymore," Mama said as she settled herself onto the garden bench. "It's been warm, this September." Her smile looked a little forced, and the light had gone from her eyes.

"Is everything alright, Mama?" Bela asked, placing her hand gently on Mama's arm.

Mama looked at her. "Yes, of course, *lapochka*. Your father is almost back to full health, it's a real miracle." She glanced back towards the house, where Bela knew her father was sleeping in the main bedroom on the lower floor.

"It's been hard on you, though, hasn't it?" Bela asked. Did Mama catch what she really meant? If she did, she showed no sign of acknowledging it.

"Yes, of course, looking after someone who's just come out of hospital is always hard work."

"I mean…"

"I know what you meant."

They both sipped their compote. Bela glanced across to the neighbour's backyard, which was only separated from their property by a chicken wire fence. She blinked back the tears that had suddenly welled up in both eyes. Such happy memories of playing there with Zalina when they were growing up. Zalina's parents had sold the house soon after their daughter had died, and now another Circassian family lived there. Today, however, they didn't seem to be at home.

"Mama? Please talk to me. You know that I know, can't we just acknowledge that? You know that I know about Ma…"

"Never mention that woman's name!" Mama snapped, jumping half up out of her seat and spinning around towards Bela, her eyes narrow and dark, her voice betraying deep pain behind the outward anger.

"Okay, okay," Bela soothed. "But I think it would be good for you to talk about it with someone. Her son tried to murder your husband. That's got to make you angry. Why are you being so calm about it? You're acting as if this was just an unfortunate accident, nothing more."

"It's not my place to cast judgment." Mama said slowly and decisively. She gave Bela a look that meant that she really didn't want to continue this conversation. Bela sighed and gave in. One day she'd get to the bottom of whatever was going on inside Mama's mind.

"I actually came here to ask if you know anyone who lives in Moscow. I mean…" Oh dear, she'd mentioned Moscow. She was trying hard to lighten the air, but the shadow of Maria and Pavel hung over them like a dark thunder cloud. Pavel had been released a few weeks earlier and had been put on a bus back home. Papa had refused to take the matter any further and had obviously pulled strings to get the whole affair dropped. Mama now knew that Pavel and Maria were living in Moscow.

Bela took a deep breath and started again. "Michael and I were thinking of taking a break for a few days. He's only been to Moscow once, and I thought it would be fun to show him around, you know? Be tourists, go to the ballet, visit the Kremlin."

Mama's eyes brightened and her shoulders relaxed. "Oh, that sounds like a lovely idea. Would you like me to look after Angelina? She's welcome here anytime; such a sweet girl."

"Thanks, Mama, that would be great. I know she loves staying here with you. So, do you?"

"Do I what, *lapochka*?"

"Do you know anyone who lives in Moscow who we might be able to stay with? Any distant relatives? The hotels there are so expensive, and it's a bit short notice."

Mama looked at Bela in a very strange way, as if she were deciding whether to divulge the information or not. Eventually she nodded.

"Actually, yes. I have a cousin. Her name is Lida. She lives in Moscow with her husband. Perhaps she has children too by now. We haven't been in touch for years."

"Why not?"

"Well, it seems a bit silly now. She became a Christian, like your Michael. She was shunned by her family and decided to stay in Moscow after she finished her studies."

Bela nearly objected that it wasn't just Michael who was a Christian, but she held her tongue instead. Even if her family had worked out that she had converted, they had chosen to pretend that nothing had changed and never mentioned it. It was one of those situations that she felt a bit guilty about. Should she have been more upfront about her faith? She'd held back because of what had happened to Zalina, but now the moment had passed, and everybody skirted around the 'religion' issue like an invisible elephant in the room. But this? This was new information. She had a distant cousin somewhere out there who had also converted. Was she still a Christian? How wonderful it would be to talk to her about it all. Bela suddenly wanted more than anything to go and visit this Lida.

"Do you think you might be able to find some contact details for her? An address? A telephone number?"

"I'll see what I can do, *lapochka*. Now, finish your compote and come and help me get dinner ready."

Chapter 9

Azamat

Azamat came home from work to find a pair of shoes he recognised as belonging to his sister Bela. He kicked his own shoes off by the door and switched to house slippers. Bela, Mama and Madina were all in the kitchen peeling potatoes.

"Hey, little sis!" Azamat gave Bela a hug. "Good to see you. How's everyone?"

"Michael and Angelina are both well, thank you. How are things with you?"

"Good. Are you staying for dinner?"

"No, I need to get back. Angelina will be home from school soon."

Bela turned back to Madina. "I heard Alyona's dance ensemble won the regionals this year."

Madina's face flushed with pride. "Yes, they were amazing! Alyona really enjoyed it too. It's been a lot of hard work, but she loves being up there on the stage."

Madina turned to Azamat. "You would have loved it, Azamat. You used to enjoy dancing, didn't you?

You should come next time."

"It's been a long time since I've been up there on the stage," he said, his mouth turning up in a sad smile. He grabbed a stool and joined them at the table.

"Milana's son Alikhan was particularly good," Madina said, turning back to Bela. "He's got real talent, that boy."

Bela's eyebrows furrowed. "Remind me who Milana is?"

"Oh, you remember, she was my best friend from the village. She lived just down the road, and Alyona and Alikhan were playmates. He's just a year younger than Alyona."

Bela looked thoughtful. "I remember you talking about her, but I don't think we ever met."

"No, perhaps not," Madina continued, "But it's been great fun seeing them again. We bumped into each other at one of the dance practices last year and have been meeting up regularly at the café afterwards."

They hadn't seemed to notice that the colour had drained from Azamat's face at the mention of Milana. His body had frozen rigid but his mind was doing overtime.

"And do they still live in your old village?" he managed to ask, trying to keep his voice neutral. Could they see his hands shaking?

"Yes, they're still there. Alikhan goes to school number twelve, on the other side of Shekala."

Azamat shifted his chair back. Perhaps he should excuse himself. He needed space to think. But the conversation had already moved on.

"Mama, let me make dinner tonight," said Madina, rising up out of her seat. "Why don't you go and put your feet up?"

"No, no need. You go and have a rest; you must have had a long day at work."

"Oh, but Mama, I need to make my way here. Alyona and I have been living with you for several years now. I should be doing more."

"Don't be silly, *lapochka*. You work, and you pay for your food. You help enough around the kitchen. Besides, I enjoy cooking for you all."

Madina sat down on her stool again. "Musa found me," she said after a moment's silence. She glanced at Bela and Azamat, assessing their reaction.

Mama stopped what she was doing, her body frozen for a brief moment as she too absorbed the news. She returned to her chopping board, but the knife seemed to be cutting more quickly and forcefully. "What did he want?"

Azamat understood why Mama had an edge to her voice. Musa had been sleeping with other women before Alyona had even been born, and he'd asked for a divorce as soon as one of his floozies had shown an interest in a more permanent relationship. As far as Azamat knew, Musa had never bothered to check up on Alyona or tried to see to her in the seven years they'd been living here in Awush with his parents.

"I'm not sure, actually. He was courteous and polite."

"Did he ask after Alyona?"

"Yes, he did. He asked me if he could get in contact with her."

"What did you say?"

"I said I needed to talk to Alyona first, but that I had no objections myself."

"It's about time he was a proper father to that child," Mama muttered under her breath. The rhythmic sounds of the kitchen knife forcefully hitting the chopping board filled the awkward silence.

Azamat excused himself properly this time. This

was women's conversation, and he could tell his presence wasn't wanted. Mama said she would call him when dinner was ready. He slumped in the chair in front of the television but paid no attention to the show that was on.

His body and mind were tense as he thought about Madina's ex-husband. What right did he have to barge his way back into their lives after the way he'd treated them? His niece, Alyona, was so special to Azamat, he couldn't bear the thought of her having to go through all that pain again. As far as he was aware, she'd moved on and barely thought of her father anymore. She was happy now. What was this news going to do to her? What would it do to his sister, Madina? She was the happiest now that he'd seen her in a long time. How dare this man...

But then he caught himself. The irony struck him. How was he any different from Musa? Okay, he hadn't ever cheated on Milana while they were together, but he'd still walked away from his child and had made no attempt to contact him until now. He was about to do exactly the same thing. What if Alikhan was happy and carefree, and he was about to come into his life and shake everything up. Could he do that? Would he be that guy? He despised Musa, but was he any better himself, really? Perhaps it was best to drop the whole idea about trying to be reunited with his son.

Mama called out that dinner was ready. As he got up to go into the kitchen a thought struck him. School number twelve. He knew where that was. It wasn't all that far from where he worked.

Chapter 10

Milana

Milana sat in the waiting room at the clinic. She looked around her at the tiled floors, the water cooler in the corner, the immaculately dressed receptionist. This was definitely one of the best clinics in Shekala. Surely, they'd be able to tell her what was wrong.

She glanced around at the other women waiting there. They were all well-dressed. Some were heavily pregnant, others, perhaps, coming for their first ultrasound. A door opened and a young woman came out, carrying a slip of paper, relief and joy plastered all over her face. Good news, no doubt.

Her own pregnancy, fifteen, no sixteen, years ago, was a bit of a blur. It had been unexpected and then quickly hushed up while wedding plans were hastily put in place. She remembered having one ultrasound over at one of the sanatoria hotels. The doctor had announced with great pleasure that she was expecting a boy and that everything was looking healthy. Milana had been surprised to feel happy herself. As she had watched the shadowy blur on the screen moving around, suddenly her maternal instincts had kicked in. She was going to have a baby. She was going to be a mother. She might have made a few mistakes in her young life up to that point, but she'd resolved that day that she was going to be the best mother ever. Her son deserved that much.

"Who's last in line?" A new girl had come into the waiting room to join the queue. Milana put up her hand and the young woman acknowledged her and sat down.

Milana watched as another expectant mother came out of the consultation room. There were still at least another five girls ahead of her. Looking around, she suddenly felt old. She was only thirty-three, but anyone over the age of twenty-five was considered a 'geriatric mother' and treated with extra caution. She checked her bag to make sure that the results of the blood tests she'd had done last week were still there. Of course, they were. They hadn't made any sense to her, but the doctor today would hopefully tell her what the problem was. Why hadn't she been able to get pregnant a second time?

It hadn't really bothered her at all, actually. She'd been so wrapped up in Alikhan, and so proud of all his achievements. Besides, the birth process itself had been rather painful, and she hadn't been in a hurry to repeat that. Sleepless nights, sore nipples, endless changes of soiled nappies. Did she really want to go through all that again? She had been so young at the time that she hadn't wanted to have another child. It still seemed amazing that fifteen years had passed already. Was it that her biological clock was ticking now? Was that why she was here? Did she want another child before it was too late?

Perhaps, if she were honest, it wasn't so much a desire to get pregnant again that had brought her here. It was more curiosity. Why hadn't she? Her previous pregnancy and birth had been so straight-forward, there had been no indication that she had been left scarred or unable to bear another child.

Murat hadn't pressed her at all. He was a dear husband, really. She'd come to be very fond of him over the years, although she couldn't hand on heart say that she truly loved him. There had only been one man in her life who had won her heart, and he'd taken it away with him the day she let him go. No, Murat had been quite content with just the one son. In fact, the more she thought about it, the stranger it seemed that he'd never even brought up the subject of having another. She assumed he'd just been waiting for nature to take its course, but now... Why didn't he want to have more children?

"Next."

Milana looked up and realised it was her turn to go into the doctor's office. She quickly grabbed her handbag and followed the doctor into the room, closing the door behind her. She sat on the chair indicated, perching her handbag on her knees.

"You have the results of the blood tests?"

"Yes, here they are," she said, quickly handing over the slips of paper she'd been hiding from Murat for the last two days.

The doctor studied them for a few moments and then added them to the file along with the results of the ultrasound. She removed her glasses and placed them on the table before folding her arms and looking at Milana with the usual authoritative look of a person wearing a white coat.

"It would seem that everything is healthy. There's no reason why you shouldn't be able to have another baby. Have you been taking birth control?"

"Um, no, actually. Not for several years now. I

just kind of stopped after my son was about seven and in school."

"And how old is he now?"

"Fifteen."

"Oh." A frown crossed the doctor's forehead. "Has your husband been tested?"

"What? Oh, no. I don't think so."

"Well, I suggest he takes some tests himself. The problem may lie with him."

Milana couldn't get the words of the doctor out of her head the whole bus ride home. "The problem may lie with him." Could Murat be unable to have children? Could he be sterile? Did he know? It was time they sat down and had a proper talk. They might decide not to have any more children, but at least she wanted to know if they could.

Chapter 11

Bela

Moscow was just as she had remembered it, only with nicer shops and fancier restaurants. Clearly a lot of money was pouring into the place, and evidence of wealth was everywhere. It felt like a whole other world from her provincial backwater town of Shekala. There were more cars than when she'd been here twelve years ago, and the traffic was horrendous. After the initial wide-eyed wonder of it all, she'd begun to remember why she didn't want to live in Moscow permanently. The bustle, the pollution, the sheer number of people, the unfriendliness of it all. Everyone was a stranger, rushing about their own business, and no one smiled at anyone.

She and Michael were just returning from their first day of sightseeing. It had been fun to do the touristy thing. They'd gone to Red Square, taken a tour around the Kremlin buildings, visited Lenin's mausoleum and had their photo taken outside St Basil's cathedral. Bela had remembered a lovely little café down a side street, where they'd enjoyed Georgian cheese pies for lunch.

She could feel the stress of the past couple of months melting off her shoulders, and even Michael seemed happier and more relaxed.

They walked the last couple of blocks from the metro station to Lida's apartment block. Lida and her family had been wonderfully welcoming. Mama had found the phone number and given it to Bela. For some reason she hadn't wanted to speak to Lida herself. Perhaps it had been too long, or maybe she hadn't wanted to explain about how Papa was. Anyway, Bela had called up and it had all been arranged. Bela and Michael were welcome to stay as long as they liked, and the sofa bed in the living room was very comfortable.

"You're back, how was it?" Lida met them enthusiastically at the door.

"It was great, thanks, but my feet are killing me!" Bela grimaced as she removed her shoes and rubbed the soles of her feet.

"It's so great to be here. We've taken loads of photos," added Michael. Lida had been won over by his charm immediately and fussed around him like a mother hen.

"I'll get you something to eat, you must be hungry," she said, disappearing off into the kitchen.

Michael grinned at Bela. "I could get used to living here."

"Just don't expect the same level of service when we get home," Bela replied, playfully punching him in the arm.

"Can I help you with anything?" Bela asked Lida as she joined her in the kitchen.

"Yes, thank you, dear. You can cut up some bread for me. Here." She handed Bela a chopping board and a knife. Bela took the bread that was on the table and started carving it into chunks.

"My son, Daniel, will be joining us for dinner tonight."

"Your son? Oh, it would be lovely to meet him." Bela had found out soon after arriving that Lida and her husband Vladimir had a son and a daughter. More distant cousins she hadn't known about.

"Will your daughter also be coming? I'd love to meet her too."

"No, just Daniel tonight. Irina sends her apologies, she's away visiting friends. She hopes to come later in the week."

"I can't wait to meet them both."

"Yes, they're wonderful young people. Such a gift from God. We're so thankful to have them both."

Bela finished slicing the bread and started arranging some pickled cucumbers onto a plate.

"Lida, would you mind telling me a little of the story of how you came to be here? I… I can't believe I didn't know about you until just a few days ago."

Lida smiled, her eyes sad and wistful. Michael joined them at the table.

"Well, it was a long time ago now. I was living in Psydakhe, the same village where your mother was brought up, Bela. I was ten years older than her, but we often played together. Our houses were on the same street.

Times were hard, back then. I had been born just after the war, and my father came back a disturbed and haunted man. He would never talk about what had happened, but he had terrible nightmares and would regularly wake up the whole house with his screaming. The people of the Caucasus had been horribly oppressed by Stalin, though many refused to believe that he was the one who'd sent the orders and they continued to worship him as a great leader. In 1944, two years before I was born, thirty-eight thousand Balkars were deported to Central Asia in just one day, with no warning. Chechens, Ingush, Karachai. They were all deported. Accused of collaborating with the Nazis, you see."

Lida wiped a tear from her eye. "Even now it still makes me so sad."

"They came back, though, didn't they?" Bela asked.

"Yes, in 1957, just after your mother was born. But it was too late. The damage had been done. So many had died in the cattle trucks and because of the conditions when they reached their destination. It was a tragedy.

Anyway, it wasn't just ethnic people groups that were persecuted and sent away. Religion of any kind was also condemned - Christians, Muslims, Buddhists, anything. We were all taught in school that atheism was the only way and that religion was for the weak.

When the Balkars came back, one family moved into our village, just down the street. They'd brought with them an elderly woman. She was a Russian German who'd been living in Kazakhstan with her family for many years, but her family had all died, and the Balkar family had been touched by her kindness to them and brought her back to look after her. She was a Christian, but not the Orthodox kind that I had heard about. She was the most wonderful lady. So kind and patient. She had a beautiful spirit. She'd forgiven all that had happened to her, which we just couldn't understand. How could you forgive the people who'd done such terrible things to your family? But it gave her a peace that no one else in our village seemed to have.

I spent a lot of time with her. Helping her with simple chores and listening to her stories. She told me stories of the Bible. She told me about Jesus. I couldn't believe I'd never heard about those things before, they were wonderful."

"So, you became a Christian?" asked Bela, transfixed by the story that was unfolding.

Lida smiled. "Yes. Yes, I did."

"But it wasn't taken well by your family, I suppose," said Michael, who seemed equally absorbed in the story.

"No, of course. It was to be expected. My parents were so worried about what would happen if people found out. I had to keep it quiet and not tell anyone."

"That must have been difficult," said Bela.

"Yes, but I was given courage knowing what the old lady had gone through, and at least I could talk to her openly. She taught me a lot about what it meant to be a follower of Jesus."

"So, what did you do next?" asked Bela.

"Well, my studies brought me here to Moscow and I just decided it was best for everyone if I stayed. It wasn't easy being a Christian here in Moscow either, but there were more of us. I met my husband, Vladimir, got married and settled down. I asked God to show me how I could serve Him here in Moscow, and He led me to work at the orphanage. I've been working there now for... Oh, let me see, since 1972. How long is that?"

"Thirty-eight years," said Michael.

"Oh my, is it really that long?" Lida's eyes sparkled and she took a bite of a pickled cucumber.

"And your children, when were they born?" asked Bela. She still couldn't believe she'd never heard about Lida and her story before.

"Oh, Daniel came along just a few months after I started working at the orphanage. A real blessing from God." Lida focussed her eyes on her teacup rather intently. "And we got Irina about a year later."

Lida's choice of words and mannerisms seemed a

little strange. Perhaps there was more to that particular story, but just as Bela was going to probe further the doorbell rang.

"That must be Daniel!" Lida's face lit up and she rushed over to open the door. Bela and Michael hung back, waiting to be introduced. Soon, a tall, dark-eyed man with a kind face and wisps of grey hair amidst the dark brown entered the kitchen and shook hands with Michael and Bela. He had a warm smile, and Bela could detect a family resemblance. He was, after all, related to her, albeit somewhat distantly.

"It's so good to meet you both," Daniel said warmly. "Mother's told me a lot about you on the phone. She's so excited that you're staying here for a while."

Daniel sat down in the chair that Lida had offered him, and his mother hurried to fetch him a plate full of food.

Bela and Michael chatted easily with Daniel for a while, filling him in on the story of how they met and a little about Michael's background. Bela answered questions about her family back home.

"We're so sorry to hear about your father. Is he recovering well?" Daniel seemed genuinely concerned. Perhaps he knew as little about Bela's family as she had known about his.

"Yes, thank you, the doctors say he'll make a full recovery. It's a miracle, really. God must have been watching over him."

"Yes."

In that one word, Bela could tell immediately that Daniel, too, was a believer, a follower of Jesus. How wonderful to have relatives who shared her faith. She was so looking forward to getting to know them better. She'd been having so many doubts in recent months, but now, here in Moscow, she felt her faith strengthening and her doubts dissipating. If only they could stay here longer, but they'd promised Mama only to be gone a week, and she was missing Angelina terribly.

Later that night, as Bela and Michael were settling down to sleep on their sofa bed, Bela couldn't help but reflect on all that they'd learned about her relations that day.

"I still can't believe I didn't know about them," she said, snuggling up to Michael and wrapping her feet around his.

"They are really great people," he agreed. "Lida seems to be doing amazing work at the orphanage; I'm sure she's making a real difference to many children's lives."

"Yes," said Bela quietly, remembering all too well the day she'd gone to collect Angelina from the orphanage in Beslan. "You seemed to get on really well with Daniel," she added.

"Yeah. He was telling me all about his business."

"Oh, what does he do? I was talking to Lida at that point, I think. I missed that conversation."

"He works for an NGO involved in raising education levels amongst children from ethnic minorities. You know, trying to get more materials available in their mother tongues, since that's the language they learn in best."

"Oh, that's right up your street. Did you tell him about your research?"

"Yes, he was really interested."

"You know," Bela's thoughts had already returned to her conversation with Lida, "Lida's story about the old lady from Kazakhstan got me thinking."

"Oh? About what?"

"About how important it is to forgive."

"In what way?"

"Well, Lida told me more of the old lady's story, of all the horrible things she went through. Did you know, several of her grandchildren died of starvation during the war because some corrupt official was holding back the money that her son was sending them?"

"That's horrible."

"Yes, and yet she still forgave the official. How do you think she was able to do that?"

"Her strong faith, no doubt. And she must have learned that holding onto bitterness and unforgiveness only really hurts yourself. The Bible tells us to let go of our resentment, no matter how justified, and leave vengeance and justice up to God. One day everyone will get exactly what they deserve, and all wrongs will be put right."

Bela was silent for a while, thinking.

"You're thinking about Maria and Pavel, aren't you?" Michael guessed.

"Yes. Maria held onto her bitterness and unforgiveness for years and look what happened. Her son nearly murdered a man."

Michael gently kissed her forehead and rolled over. "Try not to think about that now. We need to get our sleep. Busy day tomorrow, walking around all the tourist sights again, and then we've got the ballet in the evening."

"You're right. I hope my feet have recovered. Goodnight."

"Goodnight."

Bela kissed his cheek gently and then lay in the darkness on her back, gazing up at the ornately decorated ceiling of Lida's living room. It wasn't that easy to get those thoughts out of her head, and the more she dwelt on them, the more she wondered whether there was something she ought to do.

It was the day before they were supposed to leave. Bela was pretty sure they'd seen everything that Moscow had to offer and she was eager to get home and give Angelina a hug. However, the time away had indeed been good for her. It had taken her mind off the disappointment of not yet being pregnant and had certainly helped to put things into perspective. After spending a lot of time speaking to Lida, who was so wise, she felt more confident now about trusting God that He knew what He was doing. He understood her pain, and somehow, He was working to bring some good from what she was going through, even if she didn't understand what that was.

Bela turned the corner onto a familiar street. She'd left Michael at home chatting with Daniel, who'd come round for dinner again. She'd tried to be very casual about the way she said she was just popping out to do some last-minute shopping, but in reality, she didn't want Michael to know where she was going. Should she have told him? Maybe. But then he might have tried to talk her out of it, and once she set her mind on something, she was determined to see it through.

She slowed her footsteps as she neared the building she was heading for. There it was. Unchanged since the last time she was here, eleven years ago. Her skin prickled underneath her coat and her stomach started to tighten. She stopped outside the main entrance. Perhaps this was a stupid idea. Perhaps it was dangerous too. She remembered how Pavel had looked at her in the police holding room. Would he be here? This was where his mother lived, but maybe he hadn't come back home? There was no guarantee that Maria even still lived there anymore.

The door opened and one of the residents came out of the building. Instinctively, Bela grabbed the door before it slammed shut and stepped inside. She was here now. There were the same, grimy mailboxes where she'd encountered Maria all those years ago. She shuddered, thinking about the look of desperation that had been in Maria's eyes.

Without really knowing what she was doing, she started climbing the stairs. She still remembered the exact address after all those months of delivering Papa's envelopes full of money.

She found the door on the fourth floor and took a deep breath. *Here goes!* She rang the doorbell. Silence. Oh, thank goodness, no one was home. This was a stupid idea after all. What was she thinking? She waited a few seconds more, then turned to start going back down the stairs. But at that moment, the door opened.

A thin, pale woman stood before her, and they stared at each other for a moment. Bela knew she should say something, but her tongue seemed to be stuck in her throat.

"It's you, isn't it? Aslan's girl. What do you want?"

"I…um… I just wanted to talk. Can I come in?"

Maria eyed her for several seconds and then slowly pulled the door further open to allow Bela to pass through. "If you must."

Bela entered the apartment. It was shabby and dark. The furniture was old and worn, and the place seemed devoid of any beauty. A couple of sad, drooping plants sat on the windowsill of the living room, where Maria had indicated they should go. Bela looked around and chose to sit down on the end of the only sofa. She perched on the edge, feeling decidedly awkward. What was she doing here again? She hadn't even properly rehearsed what she'd wanted to say.

Maria sat herself down on a little stool near the doorway and waited for Bela to speak. Bela was about to open with some polite comment about the apartment but stopped short since there really was nothing nice to say about it.

She took another deep breath, gathered her courage and shot up a quick prayer to God to give her the right words to say. She straightened her back and tried to smile.

"How's Pavel?"

"He's not here. What do you want with him?"

"I… I just wanted to know if he was okay."

Maria snorted a laugh. "Why would you want to know that? What do you care?"

"Papa wanted to let him go. I just wanted to know if he got back home okay."

Maria's look softened slightly as she remembered, no doubt, what kind of prison sentence her son would have faced if Papa had pressed charges.

"Yes, well, we're grateful it wasn't taken further. He got back fine."

"Do you know why he did it? I mean, why was he so angry that he wanted to kill my father."

Maria's eyes flashed defiantly again. "I brought him up to know exactly what kind of man his father was, and how he'd abandoned us. I… I didn't mean for him to try to kill him though. I didn't think it would go that far. I just wanted him to hate him, that's all."

"And you? Do you still hate my father, after all these years?"

Maria twiddled the hem of her old woollen cardigan before looking Bela in the eyes again. "He ruined my life. I'll never forgive him for that."

"But surely you can see that all this hate you have towards my father is only hurting you. Hurting Pavel. Isn't it time you forgave and moved on?"

"Forgave? Hah" she spat. Bela looked at the woman, her features all twisted through years of holding onto that hatred. She felt sorry for her.

"If it helps, I forgive you."

The woman looked up, confusion in her eyes. "You. Forgive me. Why?"

"I forgive you for having an affair with a man that you knew was married and had children. I forgive you for the pain you gave my mother, who knew about it. I forgive you for... for being the reason I was never able to finish my education and go to London. I forgive you for bringing up your son with so much hatred that he nearly murdered my father. There." Bela exhaled loudly. A huge weight that she hadn't known was there had been lifted from her shoulders.

"You came all this way to tell me that?"

Bela leaned forward, compassion in her voice. "Yes, but I also came here to plead with you to forgive my father. Forgive and move on. Forgive and start rebuilding your life. Yours and Pavel's."

For a moment it looked as though Maria might burst into tears, but then she steeled herself and stood up abruptly.

"I think you've been here long enough. You should leave."

Bela hesitated, but Maria didn't flinch. Reluctantly she rose from her seat and went out to the hallway to put her shoes and coat back on. Maria waited in silence, her eyes cold, her body rigid. Bela stepped out into the corridor and turned to say goodbye, but Maria had already closed the door in her face.

Chapter 12

Azamat

Azamat stored the last of the bikes at the back of the shop and locked the stockroom door. It had been a great season. They'd had double the number of customers hiring bikes to ride in the park compared to last year, and interest in the sport was definitely growing. The race they had organised had been a wonderful success, attracting great interest and new clients, as well as extra money through tourism and advertising. The town administration had already given them permission to host it again next year. But now in October the weather was just turning too cold, and no one had hired anything for more than a week now. The season was over, but the business had done well. He'd been going over the accounts with Cody last week, and the American had suggested that it might be time to hire a shop assistant ready for the start of the next season. There was enough money now to pay for an extra staff member. Azamat could find someone over the winter, and Cody would just need to sit in on the interview process to make sure he was happy with

Azamat's choice.

Azamat smiled to himself as he sank down into his chair and looked around the shop. He leaned back and ran his hands through his hair. Things were looking up for old Azamat. Who would have thought it?

Things were looking up in other areas too. He'd actually caught a glimpse of his son, Alikhan. After Madina had told him that Alikhan went to school number twelve, Azamat had been hanging around near the entrance for several days. He felt a bit creepy, but he was desperate to catch a glimpse of his son. He could have gone to Milana's village, but his presence would have been immediately noticed. Nothing escaped the watchful eyes of those village *babushkas*, the elderly ladies who spent their days sitting on the wooden benches outside their front gates, watching the comings and goings of the whole village. But here, in town, he was able to blend in with the shoppers and parents loitering around on the street.

A few days later his patience had been rewarded. He recognised Milana as she stepped out of a taxi and walked over to wait by the school gate for her son. Azamat's heart had nearly stopped inside his chest when he saw her. It had been sixteen years, but she was still every bit as beautiful as he remembered her. The ache that used to haunt his soul returned in full force. Perhaps he was being stupid, opening up old wounds. He'd spent years in the army trying to forget her. Unsuccessfully.

He was still gazing at her when he noticed a boy of about fifteen come up to her and greet her in the understated way that teenage boys do. There was no doubt about it, that was his son. His son! His own flesh and blood. He looked so like Azamat himself looked in those family photos taken when he was younger. But the boy had Milana's graceful physique and oval face. He was so beautiful. His son! Azamat glanced around to see if anyone was looking strangely at him, but it didn't seem as if anyone had noticed. He stuck his hand in his pocket. It was shaking. He looked back over at Milana and Alikhan. They were leaving now, stepping back into the taxi that had waited, ready to whisk them back to the village, probably. Azamat followed them with his eyes for as long as he could. When they had disappeared, he felt bereft. A huge heaviness lay on his heart. He'd known then that he would have to see his son again. He was done with waiting in the wings. He wanted to be part of Alikhan's life now. But how?

That had been a week ago. Today, as every day, Azamat would be waiting on the other side of the road, opposite the school gate, hoping to catch another glimpse of his son. He locked the shop behind him and began to walk purposefully in the direction of Alikhan's school, a route that he could have done blindfolded now. Twenty minutes later he reached his usual place behind the tree and waited.

Milana didn't pick up her son every day. Some days Alikhan caught a *marshroutka*. Other days he hung around with some friends for a while. Today, though, Azamat watched him as he rushed out of the school and headed off in the direction of the town centre.

Azamat followed at a distance. He hoped no one would see him following the boy. He didn't want to be answering questions in a police station, or have Milana find out, but he couldn't help wanting to know all about his son. What did he like to do? Where did he like to hang out? Who were his best friends?

Alikhan crossed over the main road, and Azamat did the same a few seconds later. The boy didn't seem to know he was being followed. Soon it was clear that he was heading for the town park. Azamat smiled. That had been one of his favourite places to hang out too, when he'd been Alikhan's age. In fact, that's where he and Milana had met and started seeing each other. Perhaps Alikhan was also off to see a girl?

Alikhan stopped near one of the central fountains and looked about. Azamat quickly sunk down onto a bench a fair distance away and pretended to look at his phone. After a while a young girl walked up. Alikhan broke into a huge smile at the sight of her. Azamat grinned to himself. A girlfriend. Or if not, then Alikhan certainly wanted her to be. He couldn't see her face yet, but she was probably very pretty. It was funny watching Alikhan. He had so many of the same mannerisms. He looked just like Azamat had looked when he was courting girls. Yes, there was no doubt about it, the boy really liked this girl. But perhaps they weren't together yet. He could still only see the girl's back, but there was something familiar about her. He squinted to get a better look, but suddenly the pair turned. Azamat dropped his head down quickly and studied his phone even harder. He was aware that they were walking in his direction. He mustn't be discovered.

"Uncle Azamat! What are you doing here?"

Azamat looked up straight into the face of his niece, Alyona. A wave of shock broke over his whole body and he felt the blood drain from his face. He looked at Alikhan and then back at Alyona and then back at Alikhan. What? It couldn't be? The girl that his son was meeting was none other than Alyona?

"Um… hi," he stammered.

Alyona laughed. "This is my friend, Alikhan."

Azamat stood up and shook Alikhan by the hand. He hoped the boy didn't notice the slight tremble in his fingers. This was an auspicious moment. He was actually touching his son for the first time. Shaking his hand, looking into his eyes. The boy had no idea who he was, that much was clear. Neither, of course, did Alyona.

"Hello," said Alikhan.

Azamat suddenly found that no words were coming out of his mouth. He opened and closed it like a fish.

"Well, see you later, Uncle Az," said Alyona cheerily. She took Alikhan's hand and pulled him away, further down the path.

Azamat fell back onto the bench in complete disbelief. He'd shaken hands with his own son. He'd never thought he would actually talk to the boy. He'd just been following from a distance. He'd been totally unprepared for any opportunity to actually talk to him. He let out a small laugh of disbelief. He'd actually been introduced to his own son.

But there was something else, and Azamat's smile quickly disappeared as his brain whirred through all the ramifications of what had just happened. Alikhan was clearly falling in love with Alyona. It all made sense. They'd grown up together, they danced together. But what Alikhan didn't know, and what Azamat was going to have to break to them both, was that Alyona was in fact his first cousin. There was no way they would be allowed to be together romantically. He had a duty to stop this relationship before it got too far. It wasn't too late yet. He could tell Madina, but no. Then his secret would be out, and his whole family would know. He wasn't ready for that yet. Besides, she would then know Milana's secret too: that her husband was not Alikhan's real father. It was possible that Milana hadn't told anyone, including Madina, and who knows what that would do to their friendship? No, it would be better if he told Milana herself, and then she could decide what to do and whether or not to tell Madina. Yes, he was going to have to find Milana and tell her. He had no choice. But then, if he told Milana he would have to admit that he'd been stalking Alikhan. Oh dear, his life was about to get so much more complicated.

Azamat sank down onto the sofa at Bela's apartment. What did that say about him, that he had to run to his little sister before he could pluck up the courage to confront his ex-girlfriend and tell her about Alyona and Alikhan? He'd always lacked courage, growing up, even after all his months in the army. Ugh, he was such a loser. Why couldn't he be strong and decisive, like Papa?

Bela returned from saying goodnight to Angelina. She turned off the light in the corridor and came to sit next to Azamat on the sofa.

"Michael won't be here for another hour or so, he's got a meeting. What's bothering you, Azamat? Do you want to talk about it?"

Azamat laughed. "Is it that obvious?"

"Of course. We both know that you're not here because of my delicious cooking, come on!"

"I like your cooking," he protested. "But yes, I'm here to get some advice about... about a tricky situation."

"Tell all!" Bela tucked her legs up under her, and turned to him, giving him her full attention.

Azamat took a deep breath. "You remember I told you that I have a son, right?"

"Yes. You told me you'd got your girlfriend pregnant, but that she'd ended up marrying someone else and telling you to have nothing to do with her or that baby. I've always felt that was so harsh." Bela touched his arm lightly.

"Well, it's got worse."

"Oh?"

"The girl I was with was called Milana."

"Milana? Do I know her?"

"No, but she's good friends with Madina."

"Oh yes," Bela's eyes lit up, "Milana. She and Madina used to live near each other in the village when Alyona was small. Their children used to play together… Oh! You mean, the boy Madina was talking about was actually your son?"

"Yes, my son. His name is Alikhan."

"Oh wow!" Bela paused to let the information sink in. "And did you know?"

"I suspected, years ago, when I first heard Madina mention a friend called Milana who had a baby. I did the maths, and the dates worked out."

"Does Madina know?"

"No, I'm pretty sure she doesn't, otherwise she would have said something."

"Okay, but how is this worse? It sounds like at least you know where your son is, now. Isn't that a good thing?"

"Well, yes, I thought so. I actually saw him." Azamat laughed. "To tell the truth, I've been stalking him."

"Really?"

"Yes. When Madina mentioned that Alikhan went to school number twelve on the other side of town I just hung around there for a few days until I saw Milana meet him at the school gate."

"And, what's he like, your son?"

"He's amazing. He's healthy, athletic. He's a dancer, you know? He looks just like me, too, I think."

"But you haven't spoken to him yet? He doesn't know about you?"

"Yes, and no. I ended up being introduced to him in the park, but he didn't have a clue who I really was."

Bela laughed. "How on earth did that happen?"

"He was with Alyona, and Alyona spotted me. I'd been watching from a distance, but my cover was blown."

"Of course, he and Alyona are friends. They dance together, don't they? Wow, this just gets more and more amazing."

"That's the problem."

"What's the problem?"

"Him and Alyona. I... I could see that he wanted to be more than friends. I could see that he really fancied her. I don't think they were a couple, but it might only be a matter of time."

"Oh." Bela's face fell. "Oh, I see. So... Alyona and Alikhan, they're actually related but they don't know it."

"Exactly."

There was silence for a moment.

"What should I do?"

"I think... I think you have to tell them. Obviously. They can't be allowed to fall in love with each other. No, you have to stop it."

"I know, but who do I tell? Suddenly, the secret will be out in the open. Everyone will know. I don't know..."

Azamat felt a stab of pain in his temple. A tension headache on the way. He lowered his voice.

"I don't know how Alikhan will react when he finds out he's my son. I don't want to lose him before I've even found him."

He swallowed, holding back the lump in his throat. He wasn't going to cry in front of his baby sister, even though she'd seen him cry on many occasions.

Bela was thoughtful. She took his hand. "Do you mind if I pray for you? This is so huge. I think we need some supernatural wisdom."

Azamat was used to Bela's talk about praying and about God. He knew she'd been a Christian now for a few years. Michael, her husband, was a Christian, so it made sense, and no one in the family questioned it, although they never spoke about it. Personally, Azamat had never really had much time for God. Not since Beslan, certainly. He'd seen what mindless religious devotion did to people, and what it made them do. He'd had a lucky escape. No, God wasn't for him. God was distant and cruel. Where was God when all those children died? Why didn't God stop it? And what had God done for him, anyway? Here he was with a son who didn't know who he was, and a girl he was still in love with after all these years who was married to someone else now. No, God wasn't for him.

But Bela looked so sincere. God seemed to be looking after her and Michael. Michael, he was a great guy. He wasn't one of those weird, religious fanatics. Perhaps this was a different kind of religion. Perhaps it wouldn't hurt just to let Bela pray for him.

"Okay, sure," he said eventually. Bela closed her eyes and bowed her head, so Azamat did the same.

"Heavenly Father," she prayed, "I lift up to you my brother Azamat. Lord, this situation is so tricky, and we don't really know what the best thing to do is. Please would you give Azamat wisdom to know how to handle it well. Please bring along the right opportunities and the right conversations with the right people at the right time. Lord, we thank you that you're in control of everything. We thank you that you're a God who can move mountains. We pray for Alikhan and Alyona, that you would prevent them from starting a romantic relationship with each other, Lord. And we pray that Alikhan will be open to accepting Azamat as his real father if and when that information comes out into the open. Please don't let him be too angry. And please give Azamat a real sense of your peace and your presence with him. We lay this whole situation into your hands. Amen."

Azamat opened his eyes. He'd never heard anyone pray like that before. It was as if his sister actually knew God personally. Was that possible? He rubbed his temple. The tension headache had gone. Perhaps he was feeling a sense of peace about it all, just as Bela had prayed.

"Thanks," he mumbled, his voice gravelly in his throat. "I... I'd better be going."

He grabbed his things, gave Bela a quick hug, and jogged down the stairwell.

"Let me know how it turns out!" he heard her call out after him.

Azamat rang up the customer's payment in his till, and watched the man disappear out of the door with his package. The bell tinkled as the door closed. It was nearly closing time. He'd just wait a little longer to see if there would be any more customers. He sat back down in his chair.

His new assistant would be starting next week. He and Cody had interviewed a few people and they'd settled on one of the candidates. A young man they both knew from various cycling tournaments they'd put on over the last few years. He was experienced and eager and would do well. It would be nice having someone else to talk to; it was getting kind of lonely just being in the shop on his own all day. It gave him too much time to think.

Of course, he'd been thinking of nothing else but the situation with Alikhan. Bela had prayed for clarity, and it seemed that the only way forward was to talk to Milana. He couldn't go to Alikhan directly. The poor boy would get such a shock, he didn't want to be the one to tell him. He couldn't warn Alyona off either, because she'd want to know why. He loved his niece, but she had a mind of her own and had always needed to know the reason behind anything before she'd obeyed, even with Mama. No, he'd have to talk to Milana. But how? Where? And how would he even begin to explain that he'd been stalking Alikhan for the past month or so without Milana knowing, after he'd promised to keep away? Besides, he would have to see her again, and that would just pour salt on his already open wound. The girl that he loved, married to someone else, and now hating him for interfering in her life once again.

There was something else that Azamat couldn't get out of his mind, either. That time that he'd spent with Bela, when she'd prayed for him. Maybe her God was real, after all? Maybe she and Michael had something that Azamat wanted in his life too. Wouldn't it be wonderful to have that kind of peace and trust? Not to feel completely on your own all the time. To believe that someone more powerful than you was looking out for you. Watching over you. But God, if he did exist, wouldn't be interested in a person like Azamat. He'd made far too many mistakes, done far too many things wrong. He'd cheated and stolen and been in trouble with the police. He'd been into drugs and alcohol. He'd slept around and got a girl pregnant, and then left her to bring their child up without him. He hadn't even tried to fight to be a part of his son's life. He'd run away from home, got involved in a terrorist organisation, and come within a hair's breadth of committing one of the most awful crimes this country had seen in decades. He'd nearly killed hundreds of children, and perhaps himself in the process. What kind of God would want to accept him? That kind of God couldn't possibly be worth following.

Azamat took his phone out of his pocket and scrolled through his contacts list to find Milana's name. He'd added it a few weeks ago when he'd found Madina's phone lying around at home. It had been a totally spontaneous thing; he didn't know why he'd done it at the time. He pressed the ring button before he had a chance to think twice. God or no God, he was on his own on this one. He'd made the mistake, and he was the one who'd have to rectify it. Even if it meant that his son would hate him for the rest of his life.

Chapter 13

Milana

Milana helped her mother-in-law wash up the last of the dishes from the evening meal. Usually she was quite chatty, but tonight her mind was elsewhere.

"Is everything alright, dear?" her mother-in-law asked, as she added a few more drops of washing up liquid to the sponge.

"What? Sorry. Um, yes, everything's fine, thank you. I have a bit of a headache. I think I'll go and lie down."

"Yes, of course. I hope it passes soon."

Milana dried her hands on the towel. She was so lovely, her mother-in-law. She was lucky, really. She knew of many friends who'd been made to feel like household servants by the matriarch of the family, but never Murat's mother. Of course, it helped that her own mother and Murat's mother had been best friends as children. But still.

She glanced into the living room and shot a meaningful look at her husband, who was sitting in a chair reading a newspaper. He got the message that she wanted to talk, and followed her into their bedroom, at the back of the house.

Milana waited until he'd sat down on the bed, and then, after a quick glance to check that her in-laws weren't lurking around nearby, she closed the door.

"Is something up? Is Alikhan okay?" Murat asked.

"Yes, yes, he's fine. It's not that."

"What is it then?"

Milana looked at her husband. He was a sweet, kind man, like his mother really. He'd been a good husband to her over the years. But had he been hiding something from her? She narrowed her eyes and clenched her jaw. She had to find out the truth.

"I went to the doctor a few weeks ago" It was a relief to finally get those words out.

"Oh, are you okay?"

Dear Murat, he really was concerned about her. She swallowed and continued. This wasn't going to be easy.

"I wanted to know why I haven't been able to get pregnant again since having Alikhan."

"Oh." From that one word Milana could tell that Murat knew something she didn't. Guilt was written all over his face.

"The doctor said there was nothing wrong with me. It must be you. Did you know?"

There was a long silence while Murat was clearly considering how he was going to tell her what he was hiding from her. He took her hand and looked deep into her eyes.

"First, I want you to know that I always loved you, Milana. Even when we were children, playing together when our mothers met up. I never wanted to hurt you."

"But?"

"But... When I was younger, I got a virus. I don't know what it was, but painful red lumps appeared all over my body, including..." He coughed, his cheeks flushing a little with embarrassment. "Including down there."

"Oh," Milana said, withdrawing her hand. She hadn't known this.

Murat continued. "When my mother took me to the doctor for a check-up a few months later, they made me stand outside in the corridor, but I listened at the door and heard everything they said. I heard the word *sterile*. I didn't know what it meant at the time, but when I was older, I had some tests done without telling my mother. They told me that, yes, I was sterile. I would never have any children."

"So, you knew? You knew before we got married, and you never told me?"

Murat looked at her, his eyes wide like a scared rabbit. "I'm sorry. I never meant to hurt you. It's just... You were already pregnant."

Milana got up from the bed and walked to the other side of the room. She turned around to face him, her arms folded tight across her middle, her eyes blazing.

"You... You used me? You knew you wouldn't be able to have a child of your own, so you thought you'd take mine?"

Murat stood up too. He took a step towards her and then thought better of it.

"It wasn't like that. You have to understand. Your parents... They were desperate to save your honour. Your reputation. I thought that if I married you then I was doing you a favour."

"Favour? Hah!"

Murat sat down again and ran his hand through his hair. "This is coming out all wrong." He looked at her again, and she could see the pain and anguish in his eyes. "I love you, Milana. I've always wanted what was best for you. I thought maybe you'd be happy with just one child. I tried hard to provide for you and Alikhan. I've loved him like he was my own." Murat looked up, his eyes suddenly wide with panic. "He doesn't know, does he?"

"No, no." Milana sat back down again, her anger dissipating. "He doesn't know. That was the deal, remember?"

"I appreciate that. I know it's been hard." He started reaching for her hand but changed his mind. Instead he placed his hands back on his knees and rubbed them up and down nervously.

"But why didn't you tell me?" Milana felt completely shell-shocked. How had it taken so long for her to find this out?

"I was afraid we'd end up having a fight, like this one." He laughed a little.

Milana thought for a while. "And your parents? Did they know? Is that why they've been so nice to me, because they knew that they were resigning me to a life with just one child?" Her heart was beating faster again.

"No, I mean, obviously they suspected at some level, but that's not the reason. They really like you."

Milana stood up again and walked over to the window. She fiddled with the hem of the net curtain. "I can't believe no one told me. All these years, you've just let me think that we might have another baby, but now I know we can't."

"I didn't know you wanted another baby."

When Murat spoke those words, a strong desire welled up in Milana's body. She did want another baby.

So badly. She had just always assumed she could, but now? Now, that was it. She was just an old maid with only grandchildren to look forward to.

"Milana?" Murat still looked terrified. Suddenly she knew she had the power to leave him if she wanted to. Once people knew the reason, no one would question her. A quick, quiet divorce. Then she could start again with someone else. But did she want to start again with someone else?

"I'm so confused. This is all such a shock. I need to think." She felt queasy, like she was about to vomit.

"Yes, of course." Murat stood up. "I'll leave you in peace." He walked out, shutting the door gently behind him. Milana waited a moment and then gave a muffled cry of rage and punched the pillow beside her. Arghh, she was so angry! How could he do this to her? How could he lie to her all these years? She'd never really loved him, but she'd respected him at least. Liked him, even. But now? She hated him for playing her like a fool.

Milana had never been to Madina's workplace before. Madina worked for a solicitor's firm as a secretary. She had had to go to college and get some more qualifications, but she'd been motivated to start her life over again properly after Musa left her. Good for her, thought Milana as she looked around the smart office space. It seemed like a nice working environment, and the people were friendly.

"See you tomorrow, Madina," said a kind-looking man in a dark suit. His eyes smiled warmly at Madina, as she smiled back and gathered her things into her handbag.

"Hi Milana!" she said as she walked over to where Milana was waiting by the door. "Sorry about that.

I just had a couple of things to finish off. Are we still on for coffee?"

"Of course, and no problem. I like it here," said Milana, giving another approving glance around the room.

"Yes, it's a great place to work," Madina replied. "I can't believe I've been here nearly a year already."

They walked to one of their favourite cafés just a couple of blocks down the road, near the main town square. They chose a table near the window and Milana ordered two cappuccinos. She still wasn't sure what she was going to tell her friend. Should she mention the test results and the recent revelation from her husband, or would that be a betrayal? Perhaps she shouldn't be talking openly about those kinds of issues, even with a close friend. But it would be good to get it out into the open. Her mind had been so anxious just thinking about it all over the past week or so.

"I met up with Musa," announced Madina, suddenly. Milana put thoughts of sterile husbands to one side and leaned in to hear more from her friend.

"What? When? Where?"

"Yesterday. In a neutral place. Another café in town. It was his suggestion." Madina fiddled with her napkin.

"And? How did it go?" asked Milana.

"It went okay. Fortunately, there was no one there who knew us. I couldn't bear it if the gossip started again."

Milana put her hand on top of Madina's and gave it a sympathetic squeeze. "It was really brave of you."

Madina let out a big sigh. "I know. I spent seven years trying to rebuild my life and move on. I refuse to let that man affect me again."

"Absolutely. Was Alyona there too?"

"Yes. She was nervous, the poor thing. But who can blame her? She hasn't seen her father for years and then he suddenly turns up out of the blue." Madina's dark eyes flashed with indignation.

"So, what did he say?"

"He said," Madina mimicked Musa's voice, "I shouldn't have just walked away from you like that, Alyona, I'm sorry. I was hoping you might give me another chance. You are my daughter. I want to make it up to you." She laughed cynically.

"Really?" Milana felt almost as indignant as Madina did.

"Yes. Apparently, he was at the regional dance finals and watched Alyona dance. He told her how proud he was of her, as if he had anything to do with it."

"So, he turned on the charm, did he. And did she fall for it?" Milana asked.

"Yes, I think she did. I mean, what young girl doesn't want to make her father proud? He offered to take her shopping and everything."

"Oh, clever guy," Milana laughed. But then she rethought. "Well, would that be so bad?"

"I guess not," Madina admitted. "And Alyona seemed okay with it. It's just…"

"What?"

"He let it slip that he and his floozy, whatever her name is, are no longer together. Then, he offered to drive us home, but I said no because the last thing I wanted was for the village gossips to be speculating over whether we were getting back together or not. And then he said, 'Would that be so bad?' I mean, you could have knocked me over with a feather. What kind of idiot does he think I am to even consider getting back together with him?"

Milana let out a sarcastic laugh. "Imagine!"

Madina continued, leaning forward and looked at

her with a seriousness that Milana hadn't seen for a long time. "That man made me miserable, Milana. Yes, I loved him at first, or at least I thought I did. But we had, what, maybe four months of happy marriage before the cracks started to appear? I mustn't allow myself to forget the misery he put me through. The suspicions, the arguments, and then admitting the affairs and telling me he wanted a divorce. The embarrassment of having to return home. The wagging tongues, the averted eyes. 'Yes, of course, it was probably the woman's fault. That nice, young Musa, he could do no wrong, surely.' Thankfully Mama and Papa had seen right through him. They believed my stories and supported me through the divorce, but it hasn't been easy, you know, starting over again. And I'm happy now. I have a good job. Alyona's doing well. And then, well. There's Oleg."

Milana choked a little on her coffee. "Oleg? Who's Oleg. Wait, let me guess. That nice-looking man who said goodbye to you at the office?"

Madina blushed and stirred her coffee. "Yes," she admitted. "We've, um, been enjoying a little gentle flirting. It's not led to anything, yet. But at the end of the day, it all comes down to Alyona and her future, doesn't it? I still don't trust Musa, but what's best for my daughter? Please help me decide what to do!"

At that very moment Milana's phone rang from the bottom of her handbag. She unhooked her bag from the back of the chair and scrambled to find the device and cut it off before it drew too much attention from the other customers.

"Sorry," she mumbled to Madina. She located the phone and hesitated briefly as she glanced at the number that appeared on it. Unrecognised. She nearly hung up, it was probably a wrong number, but something in her made her want to answer it. She stood up and held her hand up to Madina.

"Hold that thought! I'll be back in a second. I just need to step outside, it's too noisy in here."

She walked out onto the pavement just outside the coffee shop. The phone was still ringing. She pressed the answer button, relieved to put an end at last to the irritating noise.

"Hello?"

"Hi."

The caller didn't say anything more. "Hello?" Milana said again. The voice had sounded familiar, but she couldn't place it. "Who is it?"

"It's Azamat."

The phone nearly fell out of her hand, and she just grabbed it in time. Azamat? After all this time? And just when she'd been thinking about him? Her heart started racing, and her fingers kept slipping as she scrambled to put the phone back up to her ear again.

"Azamat?" she said at last, her voice shaky. "How did you get my number?"

"I'm sorry. I found it on Madina's phone when she wasn't looking."

"Madina?" She glanced through the window at her friend who was sitting drinking her coffee on one of the tables, innocently oblivious.

"Madina. Alyona's mother. Madina is my sister. You didn't know?"

"Madina is your sister?" Milana slumped back against the wall and placed a now sweaty palm on her forehead. She took a deep breath to calm her racing heart. "Madina is your sister?" she said again. "No, I didn't know. How long ago did you make the connection?"

"A few years. She talked about her friend Milana from the village who had a son. It wasn't hard to put two and two together."

Milana swore under her breath. "Sorry, it's just, well, I didn't expect to ever hear from you again. It's a bit of a shock that's all."

"I didn't want to shock you, I'm sorry."

"No, that's okay. So, you know about Alikhan?"

"Yes. I've known for a while."

"You haven't…?"

"No, don't worry, I haven't tried to contact him or anything. I promised, remember?"

"Oh, thank goodness." Milana swore again. "So, why are you phoning?"

"I need to speak to you. It's about Alikhan. I'd rather not talk about it over the phone. Can I meet you somewhere? It's important."

"I'm not sure that's a good thing…"

"Please."

There was a real desperation in his voice. What could this be about?

"Okay. Where did you have in mind?"

"In the park? Near the entrance?"

"Azamat, I don't want to play games with you." The park was where she and Azamat had met. What did he really want? To get back together with her?

"No games, I promise. I know you're married. It's just about Alikhan. It's important. One conversation, that's all I ask."

"Okay. Tomorrow. Two thirty. Near the entrance."

"Thanks."

He hung up immediately, and she stared at the phone for several seconds. Her hands were still shaking, and her heart was beating at double the speed. What was that all about? Azamat! After all these years? What could he want to talk about that was so important?

She didn't often reach for the vodka bottle, but

she had a sudden yearning for a strong drink. If she'd been at home, she would have poured herself a shot and downed it in one go. How crazy. She and Murat hadn't been speaking for days, and now her ex-boyfriend suddenly calls up out of the blue? Should she tell Murat she was meeting him? No, maybe not. He'd been lying to her for all these years.

She looked back through the window at Madina. Should she tell her? Suddenly it felt as if her head was bursting full of secrets. It was all so confusing. When had life become so complicated? No, she wouldn't tell Madina, not just yet. So, she was Azamat's sister. How had she not known that? Well, there had been no reason to know. And Madina hadn't known, she was sure of that, otherwise she would have mentioned it. But she'd had no reason to, because Milana had never mentioned Azamat's name to anyone. She had erased him from her life, and from Alikhan's life. It was as if he hadn't existed. She looked at her now silent phone again. And yet, there he was. Just a phone call away. Just a meeting away. Despite all her intentions, good or otherwise, he was back in her life now, and she was going to have to meet him tomorrow. There was no more running from her past. It had caught up with her at last.

Chapter 14

Bela

Angelina settled into bed and Bela tucked her favourite teddy bear, Mishka, next to her, under the covers. Angelina was getting a bit old for stuffed animals, but Mishka was special. He was the only link to Angelina's real family. He'd been with her since she was a baby. Bela reverently patted Mishka on the head. She prayed a simple prayer over her adopted daughter, and together they prayed for God to bless all the people they knew. Angelina reached over and gave Bela a big hug.

"I love you, *Tyotya* Bela."

"And I love you too, *lapochka*. Now, time to go to sleep." Bela kissed her on the forehead and turned out the bedside light.

Thank you again, Lord, for bringing her into our lives. She's so precious.

Perhaps she was being greedy asking for another baby. God had already given her a beautiful angel.

She found Michael checking emails on his laptop in the living room and snuggled next to him on the sofa.

"Is that a message from Daniel? I didn't know you were in touch with him," she asked.

"Yes." Michael paused, then looked up. "He's offered me a job."

"What?"

Michael closed the lid of the laptop and placed it carefully on the coffee table. Sitting back, he looked intently at Bela.

"We had a really good talk, up in Moscow. He told me all about the organisation he works for. It's a Christian organisation, doing really great work with underprivileged children all around the world. They're looking for a linguist to help them with their education ministry. It would mean overseeing various projects producing reading materials in minority languages, going into schools, meeting with government officials. That kind of thing." His face lit up as he talked about it.

"Oh, that sounds amazing. Just like something you'd love to get involved in. Is it paid?"

"Yes, there would be a small salary. Nothing amazing, but enough to top up what we'll need once my university funding gets cut. It could be a stepping stone to other things later. I've been praying about it a lot and feel that perhaps this is the direction God is leading me. It's a great opportunity to use my gifts and talents for the good of others. The more I think about it, the more excited I get. I'm sorry I didn't tell you earlier, but I wanted to pray it through on my own for a while first, just to get some clarity."

Bela gave his hand a squeeze. "That's okay, I understand. And the email from Daniel?"

"He was just confirming that the job's mine if I want it."

"When does he need to know by?"

"I've got a week to think about it."

"Well, it sounds great. I think you should go for it," said Bela, smiling. It really did seem like the perfect fit for him. And it would be nice not to have to worry about money anymore.

Michael kissed her. "Thanks." Then he shifted a little and looked straight into her eyes once more. "I need to tell you though, there's a possibility we'd have to move to Moscow. At least for a couple of years."

Bela's heart tightened within her chest. "What? Leave Shekala? Leave home? What about Angelina? She's so happy at the moment. I don't want to turn her world upside down again. She's made friends, she's made a new life for herself here. My family, they've all accepted her. Mama loves her..." She was rambling, but she couldn't stop.

"Bela, it's okay," Michael said gently. "I've not made a final decision. These are things we need to think through together."

Bela took a deep breath and felt her stomach relax a little. "I'm not sure about it, Michael. Is there no other way? Couldn't you do the job from down here?"

"They want me to start up in the head office. You know, meet everyone, learn how things operate, be part of all the weekly meetings. But I'll double check, if you like."

"Please do." Bela's head was spinning a little as thoughts of packing up and leaving her home raced through her head. She didn't like Moscow, she never had. It was too big, too grey. Angelina wouldn't be happy there, she knew it.

Michael squeezed her hand and looked deep into her eyes. "We'll pray about it. Together. Okay?"

"Okay."

A week later Bela was no clearer about what she wanted.

"I'm afraid I'm going to have to give Daniel an answer soon. Have you thought more about it?" Michael asked one morning. Actually, she'd thought of nothing else for the past few days. She'd tried to pray about it, like Michael had suggested. Ever since being in Moscow with Lida, she'd felt her faith was stronger. She'd been reading her Bible more and been praying more too. But she'd been finding it really hard to pray about this. She knew she should be happy to do what God wanted them to do, what He thought was best, but she really, really didn't want to go. She felt like a spoiled child having a tantrum.

"I still don't know. I've been praying, really, I have, but it's so hard. This is my home, Michael."

"I know, sweetie." He came over and put his arms around her. "I want this to be a decision we make together. I don't want to force you to go if you really don't want to. But, think about it. It would only be for a few years, maybe just two. It would mean more money coming in. We could travel down here regularly to see your family. It mightn't be that bad."

"I just can't see Angelina being happy in Moscow. She has friends here. She's happy here."

"I know, but children are very resilient. She'll make new friends. Think of the opportunities she'll have there that she doesn't have here."

Bela was silent for a moment. "Do you remember when I told you about my dream? The one I had that made me decide to follow Jesus?"

"Yes, of course."

"And you remember that I felt God was telling me that my place was here with my own people?"

"Yes. But that was a choice between coming to

England with me or staying here in Russia. In the end I came here, didn't I?"

"I know, but... Maybe my place is still here, in the Caucasus, with my people."

"I've heard there are plenty of Circassians living up in Moscow. Maybe your place is with them too? Maybe God has plans for you to reach out to those people there?"

Bela looked at Michael. She hadn't thought about that. Maybe he was right. After all, it's not as if she'd found a way to serve God here in her hometown yet. Perhaps God really did have plans for her in Moscow.

"Maybe..." she said, cautiously.

"Just think about it, okay?"

"Okay." She'd pray about it tomorrow while Michael was out and Angelina was at school. Perhaps... just maybe. Her period was due tomorrow. Maybe God hadn't given them a baby yet because he wanted them to move to Moscow. That would make sense, wouldn't it? She almost certainly wouldn't have gone if she was pregnant. She would want to have the baby here, in familiar surroundings. Perhaps this was all part of God's plan? She wasn't sure if it was correct to think this way, but perhaps if her period came tomorrow, that is, if she still wasn't pregnant, then it would be a sign that she was supposed to go to Moscow. Wouldn't it? She felt more at peace than she had in a long time. At last, this might be a reason why God hadn't blessed them with a baby yet.

Chapter 15

Azamat

Azamat sat on the edge of the bench, one leg bouncing up and down as if all his excess, nervous energy was concentrated in that one place. His eyes scanned the people entering the park. Where was she? Was she coming? Perhaps she'd changed her mind.

Then he saw her.

She glanced around the park, and after a few seconds their eyes met. In that brief moment, all the old feelings came flooding back into Azamat's body and he felt like he'd been hit in the chest. It was just like in the old days, when they would meet here together, his heart jubilant every time he saw her. Only this time she wasn't smiling.

He stood up and waited for her to approach.

"Hi."

"Hi."

She fumbled with her bag and looked around nervously.

"Do you want to walk or talk sitting down?" he

asked.

"Let's sit down."

He sat down again, and she sat too, leaving a gap between them. There'd never been a gap between them when they used to meet here before, when they were younger. The gap between them now might as well have been the length of the whole park. It was a sharp reminder that life had moved on. They had moved on.

"How are you?" he asked. Would she want to chit-chat? How do you catch up on sixteen years in just a couple of minutes?

"Okay, thanks. You?"

Her manner was short and brusque. He could tell she was almost as nervous as he was.

"Good, yeah."

"Look, I don't have long. I have to pick up my son, from school."

"Alikhan?"

"Yes. Alikhan. Of course, Alikhan. I only have one son. Look, you said you had something important to say?"

Azamat took a deep breath. This wasn't going to be easy.

"You know Alyona, my niece. Madina's daughter?"

"Yes?"

"Well, I've seen them together, in the park."

Milana laughed. Her face relaxed and her features changed. She looked more like the carefree, happy Milana he used to know. "Of course, they're friends. They've known each other since they were babies."

Azamat didn't laugh back. "I don't think they're just friends. I think it might turn into something more."

"What? No, I don't think so. What makes you say that?" Milana clearly still hadn't put two and two together. She stopped smiling and concern flashed across her face. "Did you talk to Alikhan?"

"No, no, don't worry. But I could see it in his eyes. Look, Milana, I've kept my distance like I promised, but, whether you like it or not, Alikhan is my son. My own flesh and blood. I saw the way he looked at Alyona. I saw the longing in his eyes. It was like looking in the mirror at a younger version of myself. I just wanted to make sure that you knew."

"So I can put a stop to it?"

"Of course, yes! They're cousins, for goodness sake. First cousins at that. And they don't know. They don't know that they can't be together. It's not allowed, you know that."

Milana slumped and visibly softened. "You're right, yes. I'll have a chat. I should have noticed. I didn't think it all through when you told me yesterday that Madina was your sister. It's just, well, I've been a bit preoccupied lately."

"Is everything okay?"

"Yes, yes, nothing to worry about."

"Is… Is your husband treating you alright? Are you happy?"

Azamat wasn't sure why he'd asked that last question, but it just burst out. He still felt this responsibility to protect Milana, even though they hadn't been together for years.

"We're, um... It's just… No, I'm fine. It's just a difficult time, that's all."

"Oh, I'm sorry."

There was silence for a while. He could see the sadness in her eyes. Should he probe further? Did she want him to? It wasn't really any of his business.

"Look," he said. "I'd really like to get to know Alikhan. I know I promised to stay out of his life but, well, something happened this summer." He paused. Milana had no doubt heard that his father had got shot, but she probably didn't know who it was who had shot him. There was no point going into it all now.

He bowed his head and continued. "Anyway, it made me realise that I didn't want Alikhan growing up and hating me because I wasn't in his life. I don't want to replace your husband or anything. I guess Alikhan still believes that that's his real dad, right?"

"Yes, that's right. Alikhan believes that Murat is his father, and I don't want that to change. We had a deal." The flash in her eyes was back. Her free spirit and fiery, passionate nature had been one of the things he'd found most attractive about her. He had to get a grip. He wasn't here to get involved with her again. Focus, Azamat, focus.

"Milana, look. One day he's going to find out. It'll be an accident. Someone will slip it into conversation, or something won't add up and he'll put two and two together. It happens, you know? I just don't want him to hate me. I don't want him to think I abandoned him. Abandoned you. You know I would have married you, right? You know I wanted to be a good father."

Her eyes softened again, and she reached out a hand and placed it on his knee. Her touch sent a shock of electricity up his leg, but he tried to concentrate on the task at hand.

"I know. I'm sorry," she said at last, removing her hand. "It all happened so fast. I didn't have time to think much about what the future would bring. I didn't know what it would feel like to carry this secret around for so long. It's not been easy for me, either."

"So, can I see him? Can we tell him?"

"I don't know. I need to think about this."

It was the early hours of the morning and Azamat was sat at the kitchen table staring into his cup of coffee. It was still dark outside, but it wouldn't be long before the rest of the family would be up, and he would have to drive into town to open the bike shop. It had been a rough night, and he'd not been able to get back to sleep since being awakened at about four in the morning by a vivid dream. He had dreamed again about Papa. It was something that had happened often, since the shooting. He was in the park. He could see his father, but he couldn't get to him in time. And then the look in Pavel's face before he'd run off into the darkness. Only this time, it hadn't been Pavel's face. It had been Alikhan's. Alikhan had turned to look at him, his eyes filled with hatred and disdain. What could he do to make sure that the dream never came true? What could he do to stop his own son hating him like Pavel hated his father?

And then there was Milana. How could he still be thinking about her, aching for her, after so many years? He'd opened up so many old wounds by insisting on meeting her in the park, but he'd had no choice. He'd had to warn her about Alikhan and Alyona. And now? Oh, he wanted to be with her so badly. He was still in love with her, that much was clear.

All his life he'd been trying to get by on his own. Struggling to make something of himself. Pushing people away. Pushing God away. How crazy he was to think that he knew what he was doing with his life? Sometimes he envied Michael and Bela. They might be delusional, but it must be nice to think that there was some greater force in the universe in charge of your life, dictating how your life was going to pan out and giving you a path to follow.

He was so tired of being on his own, of trying to make his own way. He'd never been good at making decisions. How was he supposed to know what to do about Alikhan?

Pray about it, my son.

The words that had just come into his head took him so much by surprise that he looked around the room to see who might have spoken. But there was no one there. Great, he was hearing voices now, he really was going mad. Pray about it? Pray, like Bela did? She'd asked God to give him wisdom. It had sounded an easy thing to ask for when she'd said it. Maybe it wouldn't hurt to pray for wisdom about this himself. If God wasn't real, then it wouldn't make a difference. But if he was real, then, well, he sure could use some help figuring out the mess he'd got his life into.

He closed his eyes.

God, if you're there. Sorry. It's me, Azamat. Yeah, I guess you know that. Well, I'm kind of in a mess here. Again. I really want to get to know my son. What should I do? Can you tell me? I could do with a little wisdom here. I know, who am I to ask you, but for Bela's sake. You know her, right? She thinks that praying is a good thing, so here I am, just trying it. Well, let me know.

Okay, so that hadn't been so bad. Although he did feel a little crazy. He took another sip of his coffee, which was rapidly becoming too cold to be enjoyable anymore.

How was he going to get to his son? He took a deep breath, and for the first time in a long while he felt a strange feeling flood through his body. He felt lighter, as if he'd been picked up, or as if a huge weight that he'd been carrying on his shoulders had been taken away. He knew this feeling, although he didn't have it very often. The feeling was hope.

He stood up, drained the remnants of his now-cold cup of coffee and placed the mug in the sink.

God, I think you've got this. I know you're going to help me be reconciled to my son. Somehow. Thank you.

Chapter 16

Milana

Milana had walked away as fast as her high heels had allowed. She hadn't looked back once at the bench where she knew Azamat would still be sitting, watching her. She had held her head high and tried to look confident and in control. The truth was, she was far from that.

A week had gone past since their meeting, but she still couldn't stop thinking about it. When she'd seen him, even after all these years, she'd felt her body instantly and instinctively reacting to old, familiar feelings that had been pushed far, far down but never been completely replaced. It was like a fire had been pulsing through her veins again. She hadn't felt that for a long time. It wasn't like that with Murat. He was a good, steady, faithful husband, yes, but he didn't light her up the way Azamat did.

But she couldn't think about that right now. She was still processing what Azamat had told her that afternoon. Was he right? Was it time to tell Alikhan who his real father was? Panic rose up within her at the thought. She had spent all these years keeping the secret. They all had. Yes, there was a risk Alikhan would end up being angry with Azamat, but he might be angry with her too. She couldn't afford to damage the relationship she had with her one and only son. It was too great a risk.

She looked at her phone. Great, she was going to be late again. She started walking again in the direction of her son's school. She'd promised to take him shopping today for some new dancing shoes since he'd almost grown out of his old ones. She'd have to forget her conversation with Azamat for the moment and think it all through later.

But it had been so good to see him. He still looked so handsome after all these years. He still had the ability to make her heart flutter in a way that no other man, including her own husband, was able to.

Oh, Azamat. Did I make a huge mistake all those years ago? Should I have stood up to my parents? Should I have married you and not Murat?

The trees were shedding their leaves in full force now, and someone had swept together a pile of them by the roadside. Alikhan had loved playing in the autumn leaves when he was little. He'd had a happy childhood.

Whatever her feelings about Azamat, she did still need to think about what Azamat had told her. Was her son truly falling in love with his cousin without realising it? She really hadn't seen it coming, but now it made sense. Yes, she and Madina had joked about it, but she'd never actually taken it seriously. Had she been blind to a relationship that was blossoming right under her nose? A relationship that she and Madina had unwittingly fanned into flame? All those Friday nights at the Orange café. Perhaps it had been a mistake. She'd always just thought Alikhan and Alyona had been close because they were like brother and sister, but maybe there'd been something more.

But, no, it wasn't her fault. She'd had no idea that Alyona was Azamat's niece until a few days ago. But now that she did know...? She'd have to have a talk to Alikhan. But if she told him he wasn't allowed to get involved with Alyona he'd want to know why, and what would she tell him? If she just forbade him outright, with no explanation offered, he might find a way to see Alyona behind her back. It wasn't like it was with her and Azamat all those years ago. Back then, they'd hidden their relationship from her parents because they knew they wouldn't approve. Azamat was a college drop-out with no prospects. He wasn't good enough for her. Had she thought that too? Perhaps, a little. But with her son it was different. She would have been very happy for the two to get together, although they were still a bit young to be thinking about things like this. It wasn't a case of not approving of Alikhan's choice. No, it was more than that. It was rooted so deep in their culture that first cousins should never marry. In fact, neither should second, third or fourth cousins for that matter. It was dangerous and would bring disgrace and bad luck to their family.

She took a deep breath. Alikhan was going to have to know the real reason why. But how on earth would she tell him?

Chapter 17

Bela

Bela stared at the small white stick in her hand for what must have been the fiftieth time. There it was, the second red line. There were two red lines, and that could only mean one thing. She was pregnant. She really was pregnant at long last.

Her heart was doing flip-flops inside her chest. She felt like skipping round the room, giggling like a schoolgirl. It was unbelievable. She was finally pregnant.

Did she need to get a second opinion? What if the stick was wrong, a false positive? Perhaps she shouldn't get her hopes up too much. No. She would go out and buy another test and make doubly sure before she told Michael.

Michael. Moscow. What effect would this news have on their plans to move in three months' time?

Oh dear, this wasn't good. Hadn't she made an agreement with God that she would go to Moscow if she wasn't pregnant? After her bargain with God just over a month earlier, her period had started the next day, and once she'd resigned herself to the decision to move to Moscow, she'd actually started looking forward to going. It was as if she'd finally been able to relinquish her dream of having a baby, at least for now, and start living in the present moment. She'd been happier, smiling more. Michael had even said so. Maybe, ironically, that was why she'd been able to get pregnant at last, even without trying. Hadn't her friends at work said that stress and worry didn't help?

But now, God, now?

All the old doubts and fears flooded back into her mind. She'd never wanted to raise a baby in Moscow, stuck in some grey, faceless apartment, in a busy, noisy, polluted city with eleven million other people, far from her homeland, her people and her family.

God! What are you doing? Is this some kind of joke? I'm thrilled I might be pregnant. Thank you. But why now? Why would you let us start making plans to go to Moscow? You knew I didn't want to raise a baby in Moscow. I thought we had a deal.

Deals with God were probably not a good thing. She'd read the story about Gideon and his fleece, and in some way, she'd laid down a fleece of her own, but perhaps she hadn't had the right to do that.

She looked up at the clock. Michael would be home soon, with Angelina. She'd keep this news to herself until she'd taken a second test. Maybe it was all just one huge error. False positives were quite common, weren't they? A tear trickled out of one eye. It wasn't an insignificant error, if it was one. She really wanted this baby, so badly it made her stomach hurt. And somewhere, there, deep inside, just maybe, there was a tiny new life just beginning to grow.

A week had passed and she still hadn't told Michael. She was beginning to feel quite guilty about it. The second test she'd taken, just to be sure, had been positive too. And the third. But for some reason, she hadn't mentioned any of this to Michael yet. She wasn't sure why. Perhaps she didn't want to say anything in case it was bad luck. Maybe she was enjoying having this little secret. Maybe she just hadn't found the right time to tell him. He was so caught up in their plans to move to Moscow.

"Daniel's found us a great apartment, just a couple of blocks away from the office," Michael had announced to her and Angelina yesterday. "I wouldn't even need to use public transport to get to work, it's well within walking distance. It's in a great area, Bela. There's a park nearby, I really think you'll like it." He'd come home from work so excited about the future, she hadn't had the heart to tell him that she was having second thoughts again.

"And we'll be able to travel to England so much more easily. It'll just be one flight away instead of two. My parents have even talked about coming to visit us, imagine that! I've been here seven years already and they haven't once visited. Not that I blame them. Shekala airport isn't exactly on the tourist route. Can you imagine my mum on one of those rickety local planes? She'd have a heart attack before she landed."

Bela had nodded as she watched Michael from the other side of the dinner table.

"And we've already found a great school for you, sweetie," said Michael, patting Angelina on the head.

"Really? I'm not sure about it. I don't want to leave here. What if I don't have any friends?" Bela had given Angelina a sympathetic look. Were those really Angelina's fears, or was she just voicing what Bela had been thinking and perhaps communicating to her?

"You'll make new ones, don't you worry," Michael had reassured her. "There'll be loads of little girls just waiting to be friends with you, you'll see."

Bela had watched as Angelina put a forkful of food in her mouth, apparently satisfied by Michael's answer. If only it were that easy.

Bela glanced at the clock, and moved her hand to her stomach, almost unthinkingly. Perhaps it was time to tell Michael. Perhaps this morning, after he'd dropped Angelina at school. She took a deep breath and began clearing away the breakfast dishes. She needed a quick bathroom break before she started on the washing up. It was going to get worse, apparently, having to go more often. A flicker of excitement fluttered in her stomach. She was going to have a baby. It hadn't really sunk in, yet. She'd been so concerned about having to move to Moscow and telling Michael she didn't want to go anymore. She was going to have a baby. That was amazing. They should be rejoicing instead of worrying. It wasn't fair that Michael didn't know, she didn't really have a right to keep this from him. It was his baby too. Maybe he'd agree and decide they should stay in Shekala and raise the baby here, close to her family.

She sighed and reached for the toilet paper. Then she saw it. A spot of blood. No doubt about it. Her whole body froze. No, this couldn't be happening. She checked again. More blood. No, no, no!

God, not now, please! I don't want to lose this baby. I haven't even told Michael yet. Please, God, help!

It wasn't unusual, was it, to lose a bit of blood early on in the pregnancy? There was still a chance everything was okay. She should lie down and rest. Maybe all this worry had brought it on. Who could she call?

Zalina, I need you! Why aren't you here to talk to about these things? You'd know what to say!

But her best friend was dead. Bela didn't really know her other friends well enough to talk to about these kinds of things. Madina? Mama? She would have to tell Mama. But not before she'd spoken to Michael. Where was he? *Oh, God, no, not this!* Was this some sort of cruel joke? Why was this happening?

It was a very, very long half an hour before she heard the door open.

"Michael?"

"Bela? Where are you?"

"In the bedroom."

Michael came in and frowned as he saw her.

"Are you okay?"

"No, I don't think so."

She burst into tears. Michael immediately gathered her in his arms and held her close.

"What is it, what's the matter?"

"I think I'm losing the baby."

"Baby?"

"I'm pregnant. I took the test a week ago. I was going to tell you today."

"That's great…" Michael sat back for a moment, his eyes shining. But the smile faded. "Why do you think you're losing the baby?"

"I'm bleeding. Not a lot, but it's not stopping. I don't know what to do."

"You need a doctor. We should go to the doctor."

"I suppose so. There's the clinic over on Krasnaya street. I was thinking of going there for a check-up once…" She let out another sob and held her head down in her hands. "Once I'd told you the good news." She wiped the tears from her cheeks and looked around for a tissue.

Michael got up. "Come on, let's go. Hopefully it's nothing. It'll be okay. They'll know what to do. Are you able to walk?"

"Yes, I think so. It's not a lot of blood. Not at the moment, anyway."

How she got to the clinic was a bit of a blur. Her whole body was in a state of shock. She tried to pray, but couldn't get the words out, even silently. Michael was praying, she could tell by looking at him. He was holding her hand tightly and staring at the door they'd soon be going through once they were called. She was glad he was here. He'd know what to do. He could be strong for both of them.

A few minutes later, the nurse was moving the scanner over her belly as Bela lay on the bed, Michael standing by her side. They were all looking at the monitor, though Bela had no idea what they were looking for. The thing was, there was no sound. That was a bad sign, right? There should be a sound. She looked at the nurse, wide eyed, questioning. The nurse shook her head.

"There's no heartbeat. The baby is not growing. It must have died a few days ago."

Bela sank back down onto the bed, every last ounce of hope draining out of her body.

"What happens next?" Michael asked, his voice shaky.

The nurse was a little too prompt and efficient for Bela's liking. She probably saw several dead babies every day, but it didn't make it any easier for Bela.

"It's only a matter of time before the body will naturally abort the baby."

"You mean, a miscarriage?"

"Yes. Probably in a few hours. You should go home. If there are any complications, if the bleeding is heavy and doesn't stop, then call an ambulance. In the meantime, we'll book you into the hospital and call you when a place becomes available. They'll need to do another scan to make sure that everything's come out."

Bela put her jeans back on and followed Michael back out into the hallway, trying to avoid the eyes of the many happy-looking ladies in various stages of pregnancy sitting in the waiting room. They were the lucky ones. She hoped they knew how lucky they were.

Michael paid the bill and they drove home in silence. The sadness was palpable. Dashed hopes. Disappointment. Anger. How could God do this to them? She wouldn't even think about that just now. She had to prepare for the miscarriage. What would that be like? Would it be painful? Surely, any physical pain could never match the pain that was growing in her heart? The pain she'd be carrying with her for the rest of her life.

Chapter 18

Azamat

Azamat walked through the doors of the Orange Café and looked around at the people inside. He had rushed here as fast as he could after Madina had casually mentioned at home that Alyona was meeting her friend Alikhan tonight for a bite to eat. He could be wrong, but something inside him told him that Alikhan was building up the courage to ask Alyona out. Ever since the incident with Papa in the park, Azamat had learned that it was best not to ignore his intuition. But he could be wrong. He was either just about to save the day or make a huge mistake.

He spotted the teenagers over in the corner by the large pot plant and approached their table before he had time to change his mind. The two looked up straight away. There was no mistaking the flicker of an angry glare in Alikhan's eyes. Had he interrupted something? In that case, he hadn't been a moment too soon.

"Hi Uncle Azamat, what are you doing here? Are you looking for me?" Alyona's manner was breezy and cheerful. It didn't look as if Alikhan had had a chance yet to say anything to her.

"Yes," Azamat replied, trying to muster a friendly smile. "Your mother told me you'd be here."

"Is she alright? Is everything okay?" Alyona asked, concern wiping away her smile. "You look funny."

Azamat drew up an empty chair and sat down between the two of them.

"She's fine. Everyone's fine," he said, looking first at Alyona and then at Alikhan. How was he going to even begin? He'd had no time to think this through properly. He'd just run off on a whim. Totally unprepared.

"Then why are you looking so serious?"

Azamat cleared his throat. They were both looking at him, wanting an answer. How on earth was he going to tell them what they needed to know? There'd been no time to consult further with Milana. He guessed she hadn't said anything yet, otherwise Alikhan wouldn't be looking at him in that quizzical way. Azamat glanced around. Fortunately, the other customers were far enough away for their conversation not to be overheard, but he lowered his voice anyway.

"There's something I need to talk to you about."

"To me?" said Alyona.

"Actually, both of you."

"To me?" said Alikhan, his eyebrows furrowed.

Azamat took a deep breath.

"I know you'll say that it's none of my business, but just hear me out. Okay?"

"O...kay..." said Alyona, putting down her glass of soda and turning her full attention towards him.

"I don't know if you two are just friends…"

They both blushed, Alikhan more so. That was

enough to encourage Azamat to continue.

"But I just wanted to make sure that it was going to stay that way. It would be a really bad idea if... you know... if you were to get romantically involved."

Oh, this was so painful. This was only the second conversation he'd ever had with his son and already he was having to give him relationship advice. He hadn't had any preparation in parenting, and he hadn't the faintest idea what the best way to do this was.

Alyona laughed, a little defiantly.

"You're right, it's none of your business," she said, returning to her soda.

"If you can promise me that you'll just stay friends, I'll go away and leave you alone. That's all."

He looked at one and then the other. They both shuffled uncomfortably in their chairs. Neither one wanted to make that promise. Oh dear, this was bad.

"And why can't we go out with one another, if that's what we decide? Which we haven't," said Alyona.

"I can't tell you that," Azamat replied.

"Why not? Do our mothers not approve? Are we too young? What exactly are you saying?"

"Well, you are a little young, yes, but it's not that. Look, you just can't, okay."

"Why?"

"I can't tell you."

"Then we can't promise."

Oh, Alyona. His niece could be so stubborn at times.

"Look, I forbid you, okay. End of story." Azamat ran his hand through his hair. This was excruciatingly painful.

"You forbid me? You can't do that. You're not my father," Alyona said, her eyes glaring.

"No, but I am his."

There was silence. Azamat couldn't believe that those words had just tumbled out of his mouth. Alyona's defiance had triggered something deep down in Azamat, and his reply had just burst out before he'd had time to think.

"What? You're not my father." Alikhan looked at him like he was crazy.

Here we go, thought Azamat. There's no going back now. He took another deep breath and spoke slowly and clearly. "You're not allowed to go out with each other because you're related to each other. You're first cousins."

"What?" they both said at the same time.

"You're my niece, Alyona, and you, Alikhan… You're my son."

Alikhan stood up quickly, his dark eyes flashing with both anger and confusion. His sudden movement knocked over the chair behind him and it fell to the floor with a clatter that drew the attention of the other customers nearby.

"You're crazy, that's what you are. You're not my father. My father's called Murat."

"Alikhan, please, let me explain." Azamat reached out his hand and touched Alikhan's arm, but Alikhan shook it off and grabbed his coat. "Get your hands off me. I don't know you. Stay away from me."

Alikhan raced out of the café and disappeared. Azamat turned to look at Alyona.

"I think you have some explaining to do," his niece said, all matter of fact. At least she was taking the news well.

Azamat sighed. "I do. Yes. Can I get you another soda? It's a bit of a long story."

Chapter 19

Milana

Alikhan burst into the living room at home, where he found Milana and Murat watching television.

"Is everything okay, son?" asked Murat.

Alikhan snorted. "Son? Am I? Am I really?"

Milana gasped and felt the blood drain from her face. Had he told him? Had Azamat gone ahead and told Alikhan who he really was? How could he?

Murat looked confused and glanced over at Milana for support. She met his eyes, her own eyes wide with panic and fear. Their secret was finally out.

"What's happened, Alikhan? Has someone... has someone been talking to you?" she asked, trying to keep her voice calm. Perhaps there was still time to rectify the situation.

Alikhan threw himself down into the nearest chair.

"Alyona's uncle told me he was my father. Tell me he's wrong. He's wrong, isn't he?"

Alikhan looked pleadingly at Murat, but Murat's

eyes were on Milana.

"What's going on, Mama? There isn't any truth to this, is there?"

Yes, this was it. The moment she'd been dreading for fifteen years had finally come. She took a deep breath.

"Alikhan, darling, it's time we had a chat."

She looked pointedly at Murat and he left the room. It was best that she talk to Alikhan on her own. She'd have to deal with her husband's feelings later. Goodness knows what was going through his mind right now.

The talk with Alikhan didn't go well. Milana had done her best to tell the whole story. It had just seemed the easiest thing to do, to tell him the truth. She'd told him about how she and Azamat had fallen in love, about the way they were back then, young and carefree. She'd left out the details of how she'd got pregnant of course, but she'd told her son how her parents hadn't approved of the match. How it had been arranged for her to marry Murat ever since they were babies. She'd told him how Murat had known he wasn't the father, but that he'd stepped up and married her quickly so there wouldn't be too much gossip. She found herself painting Murat in a glowing light. Was that just for Alikhan's sake, or had she begun to forgive her husband and recognise once again what a good man he really was? There was no need to tell Alikhan that he'd never have a brother or sister, or to tell him the real reason Murat had jumped at the chance to get married to an already pregnant Milana.

She'd tried her best to speak well of Azamat and his role in all of this. She'd told Alikhan how it hadn't been Azamat's choice to walk away. He'd wanted to marry her and to be a father. She'd told Alikhan how his real father had gone off to be a soldier, and that he was working at the bike shop in town now. Everything Azamat had told her just the other week, when they'd met up in the park. She hadn't thought about it at the time, but he really had turned his life around. He wasn't the same drop-out, hooligan his parents had ordered her never to see again.

"Azamat would like to spend some time with you, Alikhan. Getting to know you. Do you think that's something you'd like to do?"

"Dunno. Not now."

"Okay, well, just think about it."

"What does Papa say?"

"Actually, I haven't talked to him about it yet."

"Papa's still my real father. This doesn't change anything, you know?"

"Yes, I know. Just because he's not your biological father doesn't mean he's not your real father. He's a good father."

Alikhan turned his face to the wall, his jaw set, his eyes narrow and cold. She could see he was really struggling with this.

"Alikhan, darling. There's just one more thing to think about. You and Alyona."

"Nothing's happened."

"I know. But, well. Nothing can happen. You know that, right? You're related. First cousins, no less."

"Hummpf." And with that, he'd stormed off and slammed the door behind him.

She'd let Alikhan sulk off to his room. The poor boy had such a lot to work through. She'd filled Murat in on the conversation, and he'd been relieved to hear that Alikhan still saw him as his real father. They'd had a lot to talk about, as they figured out how to move forward with this.

"But what do you think, about Azamat?" she'd asked at last. "About letting him see Alikhan?"

Murat had thought for a long time before he'd answered. "I guess I can't deny the boy a chance to know his real father. Just as long as it doesn't happen very often."

Milana had let out a sigh of relief. Her secret was finally out in the open. Alikhan knew, and so far, they were all still speaking to each other. But who knew what the future held? This was the beginning of a new chapter in their family life.

Chapter 20

Bela

Bela hugged her knees close to her chest and sank down into the sofa cushion. When was it going to lift, this feeling of emptiness? She felt numb.

The baby had miscarried, just as the nurse had said. The bleeding had got heavier that evening after they'd been to the clinic, and then there'd been a sudden rush that had her running to the bathroom. She'd stared at the toilet bowl for several long minutes. Was she really about to flush her baby down the toilet? She'd cried for a long time.

The next day she'd been booked into the hospital for an overnight stay. Fortunately, the bleeding had slowed, and there was no sign of haemorrhaging. She'd had an operation, the drugs they'd pumped into her arm making her head reel before plunging her into darkness. She'd come to just as they were placing her back on her bed, but it was several minutes before she could work out how to operate her arms so that she could pull the blanket up over herself. Didn't they know she was cold? Why couldn't she speak?

The ultrasound the next morning had shown that there was nothing left inside her womb, and after an ECG she was allowed to go home. Michael had picked her up and they'd driven home together. He was doing his best to be comforting, but she couldn't talk. She just stared out of the window. All she wanted to do was take a long, hot shower and try to wash the feel of the hospital off her body. But no matter how long she stood under the shower nozzle, she still couldn't wash her heart clean of the whole situation. The pain, the disappointment, the despair. It was all still there.

It had been a week now. Michael was still being strong for the both of them, but she knew she couldn't avoid him forever. She felt bad. It wasn't his fault. It wasn't anyone's fault. It was just one of those things.

The doorbell rang and it startled her. Then she remembered. She got up to let her visitor in.

"Hi Mama."

"Oh, *lapochka*." Her mother closed the door behind her and then enveloped Bela in a large hug.

"Tea?" Bela motioned towards the kitchen, even though she had no intention of shuffling in there and doing anything about it. Fortunately, her mother took charge.

"I'll make it. I brought you some food too."

"Mama…"

"Shhh… you look like you need some strength, girl."

It was nice that Mama was here, making a fuss of her. Bela returned to her usual place on the sofa and waited for her mother to bring her the tea.

"You'll get over it, *lapochka*." Mama patted her arm and set the cup of tea down on the coffee table.

"But when?"

"I don't know, but time heals. That's what they all say."

"Did you ever have a miscarriage, Mama?"

"No, no I didn't. But..." Mama sighed and thought a while. "I did lose a baby once."

Bela sat up straighter. She hadn't known this.

"What baby? What happened?"

"It was a long time ago. I'm not sure I should be telling you this. I haven't spoken of it for years. In fact, no, I shouldn't really say anything. Forget I mentioned it."

"Please tell me. You can't not tell me now."

Mama sighed and thought for a long time before she spoke again. When she did, her voice was softer. Mama was clearly carrying some guilt about whatever she was about to say.

"Your Papa and I got together when we were quite young. He was so handsome, you know. I couldn't believe he'd chosen me out of all the girls. I mean, I had my fair share of suitors too, but your father, he was a real catch, as you'd say. But just because we were an item, it didn't stop the other girls trying their luck with him, you know? They would flirt and flutter their eyelids at him. It made me jealous, but he seemed to laugh it off. He liked the attention. One day, I caught him kissing one of the girls that had been trying her luck with him for weeks. I was so mad! I slapped the girl round the face and stormed off. I was angry with him, too. I wanted to make him pay for cheating on me and embarrassing me like that."

Mama paused and sipped her tea, before continuing the story. Her voice was quiet and her eyes full of shame.

"I found a way to pay him back. One of the other

boys had been chasing me for a long time. I let him kiss me and... Well, it got out of hand. I honestly didn't mean for it to. I was so mad at your father I let it happen, and when I realised things were going too far, I tried to stop the boy, but he wouldn't. He wouldn't stop. He forced himself on me. And I got pregnant."

"Oh, Mama! What happened to the baby?"

"I was so ashamed. I didn't tell anyone about what had happened. I just pretended everything was okay. Your father and I made up after our fight, and we'd been back together again for a few weeks before I found out. We both knew it wasn't his. He could have chosen to have nothing to do with me. Getting pregnant out of wedlock brought huge shame to the family in those days, even more so than it does today. He said that if I got rid of it then he was still willing to marry me anyway."

"You had an abortion?"

Mama sighed. "No, no. I couldn't go through with that. No, I went away for a few months. Stayed with a relative. When the baby was born, I gave it up for adoption and returned home. Your father and I were married six months later."

"Do you know who adopted the baby?"

"No, I never found out. I never really tried to. I just wanted to forget about the whole thing and move forward with my life, my new life with your father. I was young and in love; I wasn't really thinking straight."

Bela took a few moments to let it all sink in. This was huge news. She'd known about Pavel for several years, but only now was she just finding out that she had another sibling out there somewhere.

A tear ran down Mama's left cheek, but she quickly wiped it away. Bela had rarely seen Mama cry or show any kind of emotion, really.

"And things were alright, with you and Papa? He didn't hold it against you?"

Mama laughed cynically. "No, but we had an unspoken arrangement, you see."

Bela frowned. "Oh, yes, I do see. He forgave you, and in return you turned a blind eye to his other women."

Mama nodded.

"So, you knew about Maria and Pavel? All that time?"

"Yes, of course, I'm not stupid."

There was a silence, and then Mama seemed to rally herself and put her defences back up again. "Now, come and eat this food I made you. We need to get you back on your feet again. That young husband of yours isn't going to tiptoe around you for the rest of your life."

"I know. I want to feel like my old self again, I really do. It's just... hard, you know. To forget."

Mama patted her knee.

"A mother never forgets, *lapochka*. A mother never forgets."

Mama's visit had done her good. Not that she was glad about what Mama had gone through before she married Papa, but at least it had given Bela something else to think about for the past few days. She'd been wallowing in self-pity, she knew that. Not that it wasn't right to grieve, but she owed it to Michael and Angelina to try to move on with her life.

She looked out over the large lake in the town park. She loved the view here and was glad Madina had invited her along. She hadn't been here for ages and she'd forgotten what a beautiful place it was. There was something about being out in nature that couldn't help but fill her heart with a sense of wellbeing. It was as if God was reminding her again that He was the creator of the whole world and He was in control.

The café where she was due to meet her sister was ideally situated, no wonder it was doing so well. It had almost doubled in size since last summer, and now, even on a crisp day in February, it had plenty of tables lining the pavement outside. It was a surprisingly warm day for the time of year, and Bela had chosen to sit on one of the outside tables while she waited for her sister. She pulled her phone out of her coat pocket and checked the time. She'd got here a little early. Musa would be arriving anytime now, and she didn't really want to be on her own when she met him. Would he be angry to find out Madina had invited her little sister along as a chaperone? Well, there wouldn't be much he could do about it.

Madina had told her the whole story. It was funny how being sad and vulnerable seemed to help other people open up about their own problems. Musa had arranged to meet Madina here to 'talk about the future', but Madina had felt so shaky and unsure after their conversation that she'd begged Bela to come along as moral support. Bela drew in a deep breath and looked out over the lake towards the snow-capped mountains in the distance. If her sister was seriously contemplating getting back with her wayward husband, then Bela wanted to make sure she was doing the right thing. Madina was eager to get a second opinion, and Bela was glad to offer her help. As much as Bela despised her ex-brother-in-law, deep down she hoped that he might have changed. Maybe Madina was right. If there was a chance that Alyona could have her parents back together again, wouldn't that be a good thing?

"Hello." Madina tapped her on the shoulder.

"Hey," Bela replied, getting out of her chair. The

two sisters embraced, and then Madina took a seat at the table.

"I hope you don't mind sitting out here. It's such a beautiful view. We could always go inside if you'd rather," said Bela.

"No, this is fine. It's nice to get some sun on my face." Madina glanced around. "Musa's not here yet?"

"No, not yet."

Madina laughed. "Well, that's something that hasn't changed. He's usually late. Have you ordered?"

"Not yet, but I know what I want."

"Me too. I love this café!"

"It definitely has the best view in the whole of Shekala." Bela drew her chair a bit closer and lowered her voice. "Is there anything you want me to do or say in particular?"

"No, not really. Just be normal, and then we can talk about your impressions later. I need to know that I'm not just being swept off my feet again. I need to know that I'm making a good, rational decision that would benefit both me and Alyona in the long run."

"You still find him attractive?" Bela asked.

"Yes, of course. Who wouldn't? But that's not the point, is it? I need to be objective about this. Oh, here he is."

Bela spun around in time to see Musa approaching the table. A frown briefly flitted across his handsome face, but he soon replaced it with a broad smile. Bela knew him well enough to know that the smile was fake and that he hadn't been too pleased to see her here.

"Hello, Madina. Bela, how nice to see you again, it's been a while." He gave them both a nod, started removing his winter cap but then clearly thought better of it and kept it on. He put his hands on the back of the chair nearest Madina and leaned in, smiling. "What can I get you lovely ladies?"

They both gave their orders and Musa disappeared inside.

"He might be a while, that queue is really long," observed Bela.

"That gives us time to catch up a little, then. How are you?"

They chatted about Bela's health, Alyona and Angelina, and Bela and Michael's plans to move to Moscow.

"You know," Madina said after several minutes, "I wonder if Musa needs a hand with the drinks. I'll just go and check."

"No, you stay here, I'll go. I've been sitting here longer, and my legs are starting to go numb." Bela laughed.

She stood up and made her way over to the entrance to the café. The place was full, and it took her a while before she located Musa just three people away from the front of the queue. She started walking towards him but then stopped. Something about his manner wasn't right. He was talking to a waitress nearby, but it was more than just a casual conversation. She couldn't believe it; he was flirting with her. Yes, there was no doubt about it. That special smile, his stance, the way his hand was casually placed on the back of the nearest chair, the tilt of his head. The young girl was very pretty, and she was obviously taken in by his charm. Bela could almost hear her giggling as she played with the ends of her long, dark hair. Musa reached into his pocket and drew out a card. He handed it to the girl, who turned it over in her hands for a while before smiling and putting into her pocket.

Bela turned around and went straight back

outside.

"What's the matter?" Madina asked.

"Musa. I just saw him flirting with the waitress."

"Really?" Madina's face went pale. "Are you sure?"

"Yes. I'm pretty sure he handed her his number." Bela sighed. "I'm so sorry. But at least you know now."

Madina tightened her coat around her. "It probably means nothing. I mean, I know that he's attractive. Of course, other girls will find him attractive too."

Bela looked her full in the eye. "Madina, that wasn't nothing. Do you really believe that it was just nothing? I'm telling you, he was definitely chatting her up."

Madina looked down at her lap. Bela softened her tone.

"Do you really want to get back together with him?" she said gently.

"Not really, but it would be so good for Alyona."

"But what about you? What if he cheated on you again?"

"I've tried really hard to forgive him for that, for Alyona's sake," said Madina. "We were getting along so well, the three of us. I can tell that Alyona's pleased to have him back in her life. A girl needs her father." She laughed. "Don't you Christians talk about forgiveness all the time?"

Bela took her hand and squeezed it tight.

"Madina, listen to me," Bela said sternly. "You can forgive someone, and you should forgive them, but it doesn't mean that you have to trust them again. Being forgiving doesn't mean being weak and letting people walk all over you. You can forgive Musa and still move on with your life."

Madina blinked back the tears that had been forming in her eyes. "Really?"

"Yes. Of course, I would have preferred for you to all be one happy family again, but only if Musa had really changed, and I don't think he has from what I've just seen."

"Perhaps you're right." Madina straightened up. "I don't want to be a doormat. I don't want Musa to hurt me again like he did before."

"Of course, you don't," said Bela tenderly.

"And if I don't have to get back together with Musa, then…" Madina smiled and her eyes had new life in them again.

"Then what?" Bela asked, smiling back.

"Then I have a chance to be with Oleg."

Bela tipped her head to one side. Her family was full of surprises this week. "Um… Oleg? Who, may I ask, is Oleg?"

Madina jumped up and linked her arm through Bela's. "Let's go for a walk around the lake and I'll tell you about him."

"And Musa?"

"Oh, he can enjoy our drinks with his new waitress friend." They both laughed.

Bela was still glowing after her walk in the park with Madina when she got home an hour later. Her sister had told her all about her boss and how there was a potential relationship blossoming there. She hadn't seen Madina so happy for a long time, and Oleg sounded like a nice, stable kind of guy. The kind of guy Madina deserved for a change.

"Bela, honey. Do you think we could talk about

the Moscow thing again?" Michael sat down beside her on the sofa and put his arm around her. "I don't want to push you into doing something when you're not ready, but, well, it's been a couple of weeks since…"

"Since we lost our baby."

Ouch! Why did she have to be so snappy? It wasn't his fault. She could see the hurt in his eyes.

"I'm sorry," she apologised. "I just, I just don't seem to be getting over this very quickly."

"I know, and that's okay. We need time to grieve, it's sad for the both of us."

"At least Angelina doesn't know. I felt bad not telling her the real reason I was in the hospital."

Michael intertwined his fingers with hers and ran his thumb over her wedding ring.

"I just think that a change of scene might actually be a good thing. It'll give you something else to focus on. Take your mind off other things. It might be helpful."

Bela sighed, the happiness of the afternoon in the park disappearing in a split second. She'd known this moment was coming. Michael still wanted to move to Moscow, and she had no reason now to hold him back, especially not now that Angelina was on board with the move, and even seemed excited about moving to the capital.

"Okay. What does Daniel say?"

Michael's eyes brightened and his smile returned.

"The job offer's still open, and so is the apartment they had in mind for us."

"I just don't know what I'd do, up there in Moscow."

"Well, if you wanted, there might be some role for you at Daniel's organisation. You're a minority language speaker, so I'm sure your own experience of learning at school would be helpful."

"Yeah, I'm just not sure linguistics is my thing."
She laughed. "It sounds great and all, I just don't think
it's for me."

"Well, perhaps Lida could use you at the
orphanage."

Bela's heart missed a beat. The orphanage. Why
hadn't she thought of that before? Orphaned children
were dear to her heart, especially since finding and
adopting Angelina, and she'd been so impressed by
Lida's dedication to improving the lives of these poor
children whom society so often overlooked and ignored.
Children who'd either lost or been abandoned by their
own parents. She knew what it was like to lose a child
herself now. Maybe that would help her understand a
little of what it felt like to lose a parent? Maybe she could
help place children in families who longed for a baby,
just like her. She understood that longing. She lifted her
head and smiled.

"Yes, maybe I could see myself getting involved
with that."

Michael kissed her.

"That's the happiest I've seen you look in a long
time. The sparkle is back in your eyes."

"It is?"

"Yes. I didn't want to lose you too, Bela."

They snuggled together, and Bela could feel the
anger and the pain melting away from her heart just a
little. She felt lighter and more hopeful than she had in a
while, Michael was right.

"You know, I think we should pray about it. And
in the meantime, I think I need to ask God's forgiveness,"
she said.

"You do?"

"Yes. I've been so hurt over losing the baby that I
was really angry at Him for allowing it. For hurting me."

"He didn't want that baby to die any more than you did. It was just part of life, Bela," said Michael.

"I know, I know, but it's hard to really believe that, when you're in the thick of it."

"God can turn all our pain around and make something good out of it."

"Yes, I know that in my head. It's just really hard to know that in my heart too. But I guess time will heal, that's what they all say."

Michael squeezed her hand. "And just to think, a few months ago you had no idea that Lida existed! No idea that you had a cousin in Moscow who ran an orphanage!" He stood up and started walking back to his desk.

Bela sat up straight. "Sorry, what? What did you say?"

"That, um, you had no idea you had a cousin..."

"I know, I know..."

It felt as if the blood had stopped pulsing through her veins. A cousin in Moscow who ran an orphanage. Could it be? Of course, it would be the perfect place to run to if....

If you wanted to deal with an unwanted pregnancy.

Chapter 21

Azamat

The snow in the park lay thick on the ground where the grass lay hidden beneath, but the central alleyway was clear thanks to the diligent park attendants and their supplies of grit. Azamat turned his face up to the late February sun, feeling the feeble warmth touch his skin. He could just see the peaks of the mountains behind the bare trunks and branches of the linden trees that lined the path, but there would be a better view from the top lake. He'd head up there later. It was his favourite spot to think and be alone.

But for now, he was waiting for company. It had been a couple of months since his unintended outburst to Alikhan in the café. He'd not heard from the boy since, but he'd been in touch with Milana several times by text and she had kept him updated. Alikhan had not taken it well, but she thought he was beginning to thaw.

Azamat had spent New Year with his family in Awush wondering whether next year would be different. Whether this was the last year he'd be ostracized from his

154

only son. Would it be too much to hope that next New Year he'd have an extra family member to celebrate with? He had decided against sending Alikhan a gift. He didn't want the boy to think he was trying to muscle in on the family he already had, or to replace Murat in any way. When he'd texted Milana after the New Year holiday, she'd said Alikhan was still withdrawn and thoughtful, but at least his relationship with Murat was looking stable.

But Azamat was determined not to repeat the mistakes of his father. He would give the boy some space and respect Murat's family, but he wouldn't stop pursuing his chance to get to know his son. Perhaps it was his persistence that had worn Milana down, or perhaps Alikhan had become curious about the father he'd never known, but it seemed Alikhan was willing to at least meet face to face again.

He hadn't been waiting long when he saw Milana and Alikhan approaching. Milana was wrapped in a light grey winter coat with a burgundy red scarf and long, black, high heeled winter boots. His heart tightened inside his chest. She looked amazing. Azamat focussed his eyes on Alikhan and did his best to look friendly but laid back. Inside he was trembling.

"Hi." Azamat removed his glove and reached out his hand, and Alikhan took it without hesitation. It was such an ingrained response that he probably hadn't thought about what he was doing. Alikhan quickly withdrew his hand and stuffed it back in his pocket.

"How are you?" Azamat nodded towards Milana.

"Good, thanks. You're looking well."

"You too."

The three of them started walking, awkwardly, down the central path towards the now empty fountains. Azamat asked his son about school and about dancing.

Alikhan answered stiffly and with as few words as possible. His body language suggested that he was being polite for his mother's sake, but that he wasn't ready to let this stranger into his life just yet.

It wasn't going well, but then that was to be expected. How long should he draw this out? Perhaps short and sweet would be best.

Milana's phone rang. "Excuse me, sorry." She took herself off to the side, leaving Alikhan and Azamat facing each other. Azamat was just about to ask another question about Alikhan's school, when Milana let out a loud wail.

"No, when? How is he? Where? We're coming right now."

She turned to her son, her face ashen.

"Papa's had an accident. He's in the hospital."

"What kind of accident? Is he alright?" Alikhan's eyes were wide with fear.

"He was in a car crash. Some stupid guy tried to overtake and then got hit by a truck. Papa's car was caught up in it all. I… I don't know how bad it is."

"I'll take you there right away. Which hospital?" said Azamat quickly. Milana didn't have a car, and it might take too long to hail a taxi. Azamat's car was parked just around the corner.

"The main hospital on Gornaya Street."

"Wait by the entrance and I'll come and get you." Azamat jogged off down towards where he'd left his car. It was bad timing, just when he was having a chance to talk properly to his son for the first time, but he hoped Murat was okay. He didn't feel any anger towards the guy, just because he'd married Milana. Besides, from what he'd seen, Murat had been a good father to his boy. Car crashes were quite common, but it wasn't often that he knew someone involved. How bad had it been? Not many people wore seatbelts; it wasn't the law yet in their part of the country.

He climbed into the driver's seat, started the ignition and momentarily wondered if he should start wearing a seat belt. Deciding against it for now, he drew up alongside where Milana and Alikhan were waiting, and they both clambered into the back seat. He felt a bit like a taxi driver, but that was okay. It wouldn't have been appropriate for Milana to sit in the front seat next to him when they weren't married, and Alikhan wasn't comfortable enough with him yet.

He drove as fast as he safely could to the hospital car park and was lucky to find a parking space close to the building. Milana and Alikhan hurried inside the main entrance, and he followed. He would stay as long as he was needed. The three of them quickly hired the required white coats to cover their clothes and stretched blue plastic covers over the soles of their shoes.

"Did they say which floor?" he asked Milana.

Her eyes were full of fear. "Fifth".

They took the stairs rather than wait for the lift. Azamat hung back in a corner of the corridor while Milana tried to get more information out of a passing nurse.

An hour went by. During that whole time, none of them shared more than two or three words. Milana had her arm around Alikhan and was holding him close. The poor boy looked really shaken up. Azamat observed them from a distance. He didn't belong here. It wasn't his family member involved in a car crash. He'd stay long enough to check that they were okay and then he would slip away. Perhaps Milana would need him to get something: medicines, medical supplies, food, water. He would stay for her, and for Alikhan, but he felt awkward. It was like looking in on a television soap opera, only this time the characters were real. He looked at Alikhan. Just a few months ago he'd been in the same position with his own father, not knowing whether he was going to live or die. He wanted to tell Alikhan that he knew how he felt. He wanted to help somehow, but something held him back. This wasn't the time.

The door to the room opened and a nurse spoke in a low voice to Milana. She looked round at Azamat, her gaze hopeful, and then she and Alikhan followed the nurse into the room. Her look had suggested 'You can come in with us', but Azamat hung back and waited a few seconds before he walked over to the door after them. He hung near the doorway, watching from a distance.

Murat was covered in bandages, but what was on show looked pretty beaten up. His face was red and swollen. He had his eyes closed, but must have been conscious, because Milana was talking to him, holding his hand and stroking it. Alikhan reached out a hand and patted his father's arm.

He should go. He was just in the way here.

"Um, is there anything else you need?"

Milana didn't even look at him. "No, thank you. We'll stay here for a while."

Azamat slipped back out into the corridor and made his way back down the stairs to the lobby. He handed back his white gown, threw his blue plastic shoe covers in the designated bin, and walked back outside into the fresh air. He shivered. Not because of the cold, but because hospitals gave him the creeps. His own father had been in this very hospital, and the memory of that time hung around the place like a dark cloud.

Ironically, that's what had set him out on his quest to tell Alikhan the truth. His father being shot by his own son. He hadn't wanted to risk that happening with

Alikhan, and he'd wanted to get to know him while there was still a chance. But now? Now suddenly he was racked with doubt again. Alikhan already had a father that he clearly loved dearly. And Milana had a husband. He'd witnessed first-hand the way they'd both looked at Murat, their eyes displaying both concern and affection.

No, he had no right to come in the middle of that. He had no place here. He'd done what he wanted to do: tell Alikhan the truth and assure him that he wanted to know him. He would have to leave the rest up to them now. He would walk away, and if God willed it, he would have another chance to continue that conversation with his son. But if not... well, it was just something he was going to have to live with.

Azamat drove his car out of the hospital grounds and down the road in the direction of the bike shop. He should get back to work. That's where he belonged. An immense feeling of despair washed over him like a wave crashing onto the shore. He wiped a tear away from his left eye and gripped the steering wheel harder. He felt totally empty inside. Bereft. Had he hoped too much? He'd been so near to having his son back in his life. So near. But now, it was like being back at square one. Back to normality. Back to how things were before and how they probably would always be. Azamat the loser. Azamat the shirker. Azamat the coward. Perhaps he deserved to have his son hate him. Who was he kidding to think he could turn things around? No, his son would grow up hating him, just like Pavel hated Papa. And one day, he too would have to pay for his mistake.

3

If I have a faith that can move mountains,

but do not have love,

I am nothing.

1 Corinthians 13:2

Chapter 22

Milana

Milana paid the taxi driver and watched the car drive off down the street.

"Mama?"

"Sorry."

She turned around, drew her keys out of her handbag and unlocked the large gate at the entrance to their home. The dog barked a greeting from his kennel, where he was chained up, but she took no notice. She and Alikhan made their way across the courtyard, up the steps and unlocked the front door. They shook off their shoes and put on their house slippers, and ended up, by force of habit, in the kitchen.

Murat's parents were not at home. They had taken over from her at the hospital and allowed her to bring Alikhan home so he could get some sleep before school tomorrow. She'd be back again in the morning.

"Is Papa going to be okay?"

She knew her son had been thinking about that the

whole drive home. She'd been wondering herself.

"I hope so, sweetie. I'm sure the doctors know what they're doing. He's in good hands."

"He didn't look good."

"I know. It'll take a while for him to recover, but his wounds should heal up eventually."

"How long?"

"I don't know. A while. Anyway, you should get to bed. You've got school tomorrow."

"Do I have to go?"

"Yes, you have to go. There's nothing you can do for Papa; you might as well be working on your education."

I might need you. The thought that popped into her mind surprised her. If anything happened to Murat, she would need Alikhan to look after her. Thank goodness she had a son. Sons stayed with their mothers. They would be alright, wouldn't they?

"Goodnight, Mama."

"Goodnight, sweetie."

She kissed him gently on the forehead and let him make his way down the corridor to his room. Poor Alikhan. What a shock it had been to see his father like that. His body bruised and battered.

She poured water into the kettle and put it on the stove to boil. She was exhausted, but she wouldn't be able to sleep. At least not for a while. Her mind was too active, not just trying to process the events of the day, but also trying to field all the what-ifs. She gave her shoulders a little shake. No, she couldn't think about that just yet. She had to concentrate on getting Murat better. But it hadn't looked good. The doctor had told her they wouldn't be able to save his left leg, and that they'd be scheduling the operation to have it amputated very soon.

If only he'd been wearing a seatbelt! There was

still opposition to making this a law, but she'd long been of the opinion that it would save lives.

She thumped her fist down hard on the table and sank into the nearest chair. Sobs forced their way out of her throat, though she wouldn't let them out freely for fear of alarming Alikhan. She had to be strong, for the both of them. And yet, she was overwhelmed by a great fear that she might actually lose Murat. All these years, she'd taken him for granted. Yes, they'd had a reasonably happy marriage, albeit devoid of real passion, but she'd never really believed that she loved him until now. She did love him! Not in the same way she'd loved Azamat all those years ago, but it was love, all the same. Why had it taken an accident like this for her to realise that?

Her ring tone started playing loudly from the depths of her handbag, startling her. She rummaged through her stuff trying to locate her phone. It was Azamat. Should she take the call? He probably wanted to know about Murat; it was only fair.

"Hello?"

"Hi. I hope I'm not calling too late."

"No, no, it's alright. I'm not going to sleep anytime soon. Still a bit shaken up, you know."

"What did the doctors say?"

"It's not good. His left leg was pretty mangled. They'll have to amputate."

"I'm so sorry. I hope... I hope he makes it through okay, I really do. He seems like a decent guy."

"Yes, he his. Look, Azamat..."

"Yes?"

"I'm really grateful you took us to the hospital, thank you."

"It was nothing."

"But I need to focus on getting Murat better now. You probably won't hear from me for a while. And please don't try to contact Alikhan until, you know, until his father, I mean, Murat, until Murat gets better."

"I understand, of course."

Milana closed her eyes and bowed her head. "I'm sorry Azamat."

"There's nothing to be sorry for."

"What I mean is, I'm sorry things didn't work out like we wanted all those years ago, but we've all moved on, you know? My husband needs me now, and my place is beside him, helping him get well. And Alikhan's place is here too."

"I know."

Azamat's words were short and to the point, and she could tell from the tone of his voice that this wasn't an easy conversation for him either.

"Goodbye, Azamat."

"Goodbye. Milana."

Milana hung up and then stared at the phone for a while longer.

Goodbye, Azamat.

It was three weeks since the operation, and Murat had been home for two days already. He still had a lot of bruising and swelling, but Milana knew that it was the loss of his leg that was going to take him the longest time to get over. Even if the physical scars healed quickly, the emotional ones would take time and patience, on all their parts. The doctors said it would take a while for his body to adjust to the missing limb, and Murat had told her how sometimes he felt a pain or an itch in the place where his leg would have been, which was impossible. It was just his brain playing tricks on him as it tried to realign itself to the new reality.

Milana knocked on the door and then walked in with the lunch tray. She set it down on the table next to her husband, who was lying on the sofa, propped up with pillows and covered in a blanket.

"Try to eat this. Your mother made it specially. It's your favourite."

Murat sighed and went back to staring at the ceiling. "I just don't feel hungry."

"You need to get your strength back."

"What for? So that I can be a cripple for the rest of my life?"

"It's not that bad, Murat. You'll soon get used to walking on crutches, and then the doctor mentioned the possibility of a prosthetic leg further down the line. That would be great, wouldn't it?"

"I don't see that anything's great about losing your leg."

"Well, it's better than losing your life."

She didn't mean to be sharp, but she couldn't help it. Murat was usually so calm and positive about life, she couldn't bear to see him wallowing in self-pity and despair. She wanted to help him snap out of it, but she didn't know how.

He grabbed her arm just as she was turning to leave. "I'm sorry."

Her frustration melted and she knelt down close to him, kissing his hand and then holding it close to her chest. "I know."

"You know, one good thing's come from this."

"What's that?"

"I don't know, but our relationship feels different. You're treating me... differently. I like that."

She stared at him and blinked back tears. "You don't really know what you have until you almost lose it." She kissed him gently on the forehead. "I love you. I want you to know that. And when you get better, we can start over again, you know. Make up for lost time."

"I'd like that." He smiled.

Milana frowned and pressed her hand against his forehead. "You're looking a bit flushed. I think you might have a temperature. Do you feel okay?"

"What?" Murat turned to her, his eyes vacant.

"You look like you're burning up. That's strange."

"I don't feel very good, actually. If anything, I feel cold." He shivered and pulled the blanket closer around his neck.

"Here, drink some more water." Milana handed him the glass and helped guide it to his lips. "I'll be back in a while to change your dressings, but right now I've got some chores to see to."

She would keep an eye on his temperature, but hopefully it would pass soon.

Later that afternoon she returned with a bowl of clean water and some fresh bandages. Murat was asleep, so she didn't want to disturb him, although his forehead still looked clammy. When she carefully lifted the blanket that was covering him she tried not to gasp. It was still so difficult to see the stump where his left leg had once been. She gently removed the old dressings, just as the nurses had shown her. Close to the wound, the skin was red and angry-looking. She gently dabbed around it with clean water, wiping away the pus. She wrinkled up her nose at the smell. Surely that wasn't a good sign. It was supposed to be healing, wasn't it? She'd keep an eye on it over the next couple of days.

Once she'd replaced the dressings, thrown away the old bandages and washed her hands, she knelt down again beside Murat. He turned to her and slowly opened his eyes.

"Hey, how are you feeling?"

"Tired," he replied.

She looked over at the tray of food she'd left at lunchtime. "You've not eaten anything. I'm going to have to return another tray of untouched food to your mother, and you know how upset she gets if people don't like her cooking."

Murat managed a weak smile, and she kissed his hand. Probably it was normal to lose your appetite after such a traumatic experience. Still, he needed to eat.

"Is there something else you'd like to eat? What can I get you?"

It was funny how much her perspective had shifted in just a few days. It wasn't that long ago that she was furious with her husband for not telling her he was sterile, but that didn't seem to matter at all now. The anger had gone and been replaced with a warm glow. The future looked bright for them and Alikhan all of a sudden. Murat just had to get over his injuries, and things could go back to normal. Only, they'd be better, she'd make sure of that.

She brought the food tray back to the kitchen, squirted washing up liquid onto the sponge and started running the tap. One by one she cleared and wiped the plates, rinsing them, and then placing them on the draining board. Perhaps they could go away, just the two of them. They hadn't really done anything together since their brief honeymoon, and she'd been pregnant then. It might be nice to take a trip somewhere, maybe to the mountains. She'd always wanted to stay in one of those new Alpine chalets near Mount Elbrus and take the chairlift up to the snowline.

She reached for another plate and realised she was humming. When was the last time she'd caught herself humming? She couldn't remember.

Three days later, Murat's wound was still not healing well. If anything, it was looking worse, and Milana was worried about the discharge. It looked as if an infection had set in. Murat still had a raised temperature and seemed weaker and more confused. Her mother-in-law was also concerned.

"I think we should call an ambulance," Milana said at last that afternoon, after the two women had changed the dressings again. Murat's mother nodded and picked up the phone to dial 03. Milana hurried off to pack a few things for the hospital and change her clothes.

Sitting in the back of the ambulance, a few minutes later, Milana felt the panic rising in her chest again. It wasn't meant to be like this. The worst was over, wasn't it? He was supposed to be getting better now. She shuddered at the thought of being back in the hospital again. This couldn't be happening. It wasn't fair. Not when things were just working themselves out between the two of them.

The ambulance lurched over a speed bump and Milana instinctively reached for Murat's hand, but he wasn't responding. She couldn't tell if he was still conscious or not, and that really scared her. Murat's parents were staying at home to wait for Alikhan to come back from school. They would all come to the hospital later. Milana wished with all her heart that she would have good news to tell them when they did.

The hours ticked by as she paced the familiar corridors of the town hospital. The doctor had frightened her with his brief explanation that they'd had to put Murat on an antiviral drip. Apparently, he had something called sepsis. What did that even mean? She didn't know anything. If only someone would come out and explain what was going on.

Murat's parents had arrived with Alikhan an hour later, and still they were waiting. Still no one would tell them anything. Finally, late in the evening, a white-coated doctor exited the room and made his way towards them. Milana desperately scanned his eyes, showing just above his face mask. There it was, the look that she had been dreading. The look of pity.

"No!" she cried out, having to catch herself on the wall to prevent herself from falling.

"I'm sorry," the doctor started, removing the mask from over his mouth. "We did all we could."

"But why? What happened? He was getting better! You said everything would be alright!"

"An aggressive infection had set in. He wasn't showing any signs of it when he was discharged, but it happened very quickly. There was nothing you could have done, and when he got here it was too late. I'm sorry."

The doctor turned to go back into the room, leaving Milana and the others to process the news.

"No, no, no!" was all that was screaming through Milana's head. Murat's father collapsed back into his chair, his head in his hands. Murat's mother clung onto Alikhan and wept loudly. Milana slid down the wall, squatting on the floor like she used to do as a child, her arms wrapped around her knees, gently rocking backwards and forwards.

Murat was gone. She was a widow.

Chapter 23

Azamat

Azamat hadn't been expecting a phone call from Milana after their last conversation, and he certainly hadn't been expecting what she had to tell him.

She hadn't exactly invited him to the funeral; it was more like she just wanted to let him know and leave it up to him to decide what he wanted to do. The call had been brief and business-like, but he knew her well enough to know that she was really upset. Of course, she was. She'd loved Murat.

Should he go? There was no reason for him to go. He wasn't related to Murat and didn't live in their village. The only connection was Alikhan. Should he go to show support to Alikhan, or would his presence there make things worse? The last thing he wanted to do was to make Alikhan think he was swooping in to replace the only father he'd ever known. The father he'd loved, admired and now lost forever.

He had to make a decision quickly. Funerals in the Caucasus didn't wait for anyone. The body had to be buried within twenty-four hours, and preparations were already underway.

In a split second he followed his gut and made the decision to go. He would hang back and try not to let Alikhan or Milana see him, but he wanted to be there for what would be a really significant event in the life of his son. Who knew what the future held, but Azamat still hoped beyond all hope that he and Alikhan would form some kind of relationship, even if just a formal one. He'd like to know that he'd been able to share that moment, to be able to listen to Alikhan talking about it knowing that he'd been there too. But it was more than that. He wanted to pay his respects to the man who'd fathered his son. The one who had looked after both Milana and Alikhan all these years when he wasn't able to.

He pulled his car up a couple of streets away from Milana's house, put on his flat, black cap and pulled his collar tighter around his neck. Walking briskly, he looked around to see if there was anyone who might recognise him but as soon as he rounded the corner he breathed a sigh of relief. Milana's street was teaming with people, and he would definitely be able to slip in unnoticed. Murat had come from a well-respected family and had himself been a good man with many friends. Of course, there would be a whole crowd of people willing to drop whatever they'd been doing to attend his funeral.

Azamat drew his black cap further down over his face and pushed his way through the crowd into the courtyard of Murat's family home. The women were all inside, offering their consolations to Milana and Murat's mother and other female relatives. The men were all outside, voices low and respectful, waiting for the imam to arrive to conduct the ceremony and prayers over the body before it was carried to the village cemetery.

He spotted Alikhan over in the corner by the

steps. He was being looked after by male relatives, but one look at Alikhan's face made Azamat's heart break. The boy had clearly loved Murat. What boy deserves to lose his father at that age? What a terrible trauma to have to go through. One thing was clear, it would be a long time before Alikhan would be ready for Azamat to approach him again and offer to pick up where they last left off. The boy was distraught.

Azamat held up his hands with the other men in prayer and then joined the procession out of the courtyard, following the body, which was being carried on a palate, covered in a white cloth and a blanket. He glanced up at the porch and noticed Milana's pale face watching along with the other women. Had she noticed him there? Probably not. Her eyes were too full of tears to see clearly through the mass of almost identical black caps and black jackets. As the procession wound its way down through the streets, he found an opportune moment to peel off and make his way back to his car. Murat's final burial ceremony would be a special farewell moment for Alikhan, and he didn't have a right to be there. Let the boy say farewell in peace.

Azamat slowly walked away, fingering the cap in his hands. What did this mean now? What would the future hold? It was too early to tell. He didn't want to seem callous or disrespectful, but deep in his heart, if he was willing to admit it, there was a little flicker of hope.

Chapter 24

Bela

Moscow was a grey, cold, unfeeling place. She'd been right. And yet, she'd also been wrong. Bela slipped in between the doors of the metro carriage just before they closed.

"Take care, the doors are closing. The next stop is Oktyabraskaya.*"*

She smiled. Even the automated female voice of the train tannoy was familiar to her now. She'd lived a whole year here when she was a student, but so much had changed since then. And she'd changed, too. She was no longer a determined but naïve student, desperate to travel to London and escape Russia. She was older now, with responsibilities. A wife and a mother, and an employee at the orphanage, a job she loved. But she wasn't coming from there now. It was a Thursday night, and she was on her way back from this evening's Circassian Christian meeting.

She found a seat and settled down. The stop nearest her home was a good half an hour away, but she didn't mind that. Sometimes she read, but often she used the time to pray.

God, thank you so much for the meeting we had tonight. Please help everyone get home safely, and please would Tina want to come again next week. She's a really special young girl, and I'd love to get to know her better.

Lida had mentioned the group to her a couple of months ago, soon after they'd arrived, and Bela had got involved immediately. She'd always felt that God had wanted her to be among her own people. Wasn't that why she'd turned down Michael at first? She couldn't see how they could be together when her place was among the Circassians. That's why she'd fought so hard to stay in Shekala. How could she be true to her calling unless she was in the Caucasus? But God, of course, was a God of surprises. How had she ever thought she knew best?

The group was a lovely collection of people of all ages. A few of them were students, come to study in the capital, and it was these young women that Bela felt most drawn to help and encourage in their faith. She'd learned a lot since she'd become a Christian, but having to answer other people's questions had forced her to dig deeper herself, and her own faith was growing stronger as a result. Maybe Tina would agree to meet up separately to study the Bible together?

Lida hadn't been able to come that night because she'd not been well, and Bela decided to stop by on the way home to see how she was. Lida's apartment was only a few blocks away from theirs.

The days were lengthening now that it was April, but she didn't want to be out too long after dark. She'd just be half an hour or so. Lida buzzed her in, and Bela bounded up the flights of stairs towards Lida's apartment.

"I wasn't expecting to see you."

"I just came to check on you. It's not like you to

miss a meeting, I wanted to make sure you really were sick!"

They both laughed. "I'm on the mend, but I didn't want to infect anyone. Come in. I'll make some tea."

"I can't stay long. I'm glad you're okay."

Bela slipped off her shoes and settled herself at the familiar kitchen table. They chatted about the group and what Lida had missed that evening. Lida was becoming as close to Bela as her own mother. Sometimes, Bela felt an ache in her heart that she couldn't have these kinds of conversations with Mama. It was hard being the only Christian in her immediate family.

Thinking of Mama prompted another thought in Bela's mind.

"Lida, can I ask you something?"

"Of course."

"It's about my mother."

"Yes?"

"I was just wondering. Did she ever come and visit you here in Moscow when she was younger? When she might have, um, needed some help with something?"

There was a strange look in Lida's eyes, and for a moment Bela worried she'd said something to upset her. Perhaps she shouldn't have mentioned it. Lida took a long time to answer, and when she did, her voice was more thoughtful and considered.

"She did come and visit. In the early seventies, before she married your father. Has she talked to you about it?"

"Only a few months ago. She told me she'd got pregnant by mistake and had gone to live with a cousin until the baby was born. I wondered if that cousin might have been you?"

Lida nodded. "Yes, it was me. She couldn't let her

family find out, you see. She managed to conceal it for the first three months, but then she came up here under the pretence of getting some work experience. I didn't know she'd told anyone about it. I was sworn to secrecy."

"I don't think she had, until she told me a few months back. Lida, do you know what happened to the baby? Mama said she'd put it up for adoption."

Lida got up to pour herself some more tea, and Bela couldn't see her face when she answered.

"She asked me to place the baby in the orphanage until an adoptive family was found."

"And did anyone take the baby?"

"Does your mother want to know?"

"No, I don't think so. At least, she didn't say she wanted to. I just wanted to know where my half-brother or sister might be now? I don't even know if it was a girl or a boy. Can you remember?"

Lida's eyes softened, and she placed a comforting hand on Bela's arm. "I really can't tell you more than your mother wants you to know, dear. But don't worry. Lots of our children get adopted, fortunately, although it's impossible to remember each individual case."

"I've noticed where all the records are kept at work. Now that I'm officially an employee, would it be okay if I looked through them? I could help to reorganise them at the same time," Bela offered.

There was a slight pause before Lida nodded. "Sure, of course."

Bela hurried home, mulling over in her mind what she'd learned. She'd been right, Mama had come here to have the baby. But it wasn't until she was at the entrance to her own apartment block that the thought came to her. It was impossible to remember every case, but why wouldn't Lida remember what happened to her own cousin's baby? A baby who'd been growing in Mama's womb for six months while she'd been staying with Lida. A baby she had perhaps wrenched away from Mama's hands, telling her that it was for the best? A baby that was also related to her, albeit distantly. Why would Lida, a Christian woman full of compassion, not have followed up on that baby and made sure he or she was okay?

Sorting through piles and piles of boxes at the orphanage proved to be a rather fruitless task. More than half of the records predated the orphanage's rather antiquated computer system, and so Bela had taken it upon herself to input all the details contained in those folders while she was at it. A necessary and much appreciated job, but one which set her search back by a week or two.

The thing was, she had already gone through all the records for 1970-75 and had found nothing. No suspicious record that might have been Mama. It was possible that Mama had filed under a false name, but Lida had said that they'd always been careful to obey the law correctly, so it seemed very unlikely she'd done that.

Bela had continued to trawl through and reorganise the other records, but her hopes of finding her long-lost half brother or sister were fading fast. She couldn't help but feel disappointed and frustrated.

When she went round to collect Lida for the Circassian Christian meeting late one afternoon, it was Lida's daughter, Irina, who opened the door.

"You look exhausted, Bela. Bad day?" Irina ushered Bela into the living room. "She's just getting ready, she won't be long," she added, nodding her head in the direction of the bathroom.

"Thanks, Irina. Yes, it's been a tiring couple of

weeks." Bela replied, sinking into Lida's soft and comfortable sofa. She desperately wanted to talk to Irina about it but knew it would be betraying Mama's confidence.

She and Irina had become good friends over the past month or so since Bela, Michael and Angelina had arrived in Moscow. Irina was as yet unmarried and still lived with her parents. She was a quiet and thoughtful young woman and had a strong faith like her mother. Bela was grateful for their growing friendship.

"Want to talk about it? I'm sure she'll be at least another five minutes," Irina asked, her face friendly and sympathetic.

Bela smiled at her gratefully. It would be good to talk a little. "I'm just trying to find out some information about an adoption," she said, "but all the records at the orphanage are, well, a little disordered to say the least."

"Oh, my word!" Irina laughed. "Yes, I've seen them. A bit of an administrative nightmare. I don't think I ever found mine."

"What?" Bela sat up straight.

"My records. My adoption records. I'm adopted, didn't you know?"

"Er…no. I didn't," Bela stammered.

"Oh, I thought Mama might have told you. It's okay, I found out quite a while ago."

"How?"

"It wasn't hard to work out, actually," Irina continued. "I think I first got suspicious when I noticed that there were plenty of photos of Daniel when he was just a few weeks' old, but there were none of me. When I asked my mother about it, it came out that it's because I was adopted and Daniel wasn't."

"So, how old were you when you were adopted?"

There were so many questions buzzing around in

Bela's mind that it was hard to pick just one at a time.

"I think I was about six months old. That's about the time it takes for all the paperwork to go through properly."

"Oh. And did you ever find out who your real parents were?" Bela asked, tentatively.

Irina was about to answer when Lida came into the room.

"Sorry about that, Bela. I'm ready now. Shall we go?"

"I... er... um." Bela would have done anything to be able to continue the conversation with Irina, but it would have to wait. "Sure," she said. "Let's go."

Chapter 25

Azamat

Azamat watched as a little boy fell off his tricycle, his mother running quickly to pick him up again and dust off his clothes. The family moved on, another one close behind: this time a young couple pushing a pram. The park was Azamat's favourite place in town and yet also the one that induced the most pain. He loved the peace and quiet, the trees and the wildlife. He loved feeling anonymous and being able to watch the world go by. And yet, on this sunny day in early April, the park was full of happy, loving families out for a quick stroll, and it only twisted the knife deeper into his heart that he didn't have one. Oh, what could have been if things had worked out differently? If he had been different?

He'd met up with Milana in this park, back when they were teenagers, but it was also here in this park that he'd had to let her go. And then Papa getting shot. Things had never been the same since, though perhaps that was a good thing. At least he'd made contact with Alikhan. At least he'd done his best to make amends. But look where that had got him. He hadn't heard from either Milana or Alikhan for more than two months, not since Murat's funeral. They were probably moving on with their lives. Without him.

Would Milana come back to him? Maybe. But it would be a long time before she'd be ready for a new relationship, and perhaps Alikhan would put a stop to that ever happening. Who would want a father like Azamat when they'd grown up with a father like Murat? Milana's parents had been right all those years ago to marry her off quickly.

Azamat got up from the bench where he'd been sitting and carried on walking up the central path. Instinctively he turned left, towards the old concrete structure where he used to hang out with his friends when he was younger. Where he'd got together with Milana, all those years ago. If only he could go back in time and give the younger version of himself a good shaking. He'd been so stupid and carefree back then. He'd been on a dangerous path, but he'd been blind to it. Allowing himself to be pulled along with the crowd and getting mixed up with terrorists. No, Milana had been right to walk away.

Azamat slumped down near the side of the wall and held his head in his hands. Had he ever done anything right with his life? What was the use of him existing at all? He'd never done anything great or noteworthy. He'd never amounted to much, just like his parents had warned him. How many people would come and pay their respects at his funeral?

Trust in me, for I can move the mountains.

Azamat stood up with a jolt. It was almost as if someone had spoken those words aloud, right there and then. He spun around but there was no one. Great! He was hearing voices again!

Trust in me, for I can move the mountains. That sounded familiar. Hadn't Bela said something like that when she'd prayed for him all those months ago. Yes, she'd thanked God that he was a God who could move the mountains. It had seemed a rather strange thing for her to say at the time. Move the mountains? How ridiculous.

But had God just spoken to him?

A strange, peaceful sensation flooded through Azamat's limbs. If God had spoken to him, then he wasn't a loser. He wasn't a nobody with no purpose in life. Maybe, just maybe, God had plans for him. What did he have to do? Trust in God and He would move the mountains?

But something was stopping him. Something cold and painful deep in his heart. It was anger and self-pity and despair and self-loathing all mixed up together. He needed to get rid of that if he was ever going to be able to make something of his life. How could he do that?

Forgiveness.

That was it, forgiveness. That's what Michael had said.

"Don't leave it too late to forgive yourself for your past mistakes, Azamat. Forgive and let go." That's what Michael had told him, although he hadn't really understood what he meant at the time.

But before he could forgive himself, he needed to know that God had forgiven him, surely? Could he do that? Could he ask God to forgive him? Bela and Michael had once told him that all he had to do was pray and ask for forgiveness, but he'd laughed it off at the time. He wasn't going to become a Christian like them anytime soon. That's what he'd told them. Besides, why would God want to forgive someone like Azamat?

But right now, he needed forgiveness more than anything. Was it that simple? Azamat racked his brains to try to remember the conversation they'd had in more detail. He glanced around to check he was still alone and then bowed his head.

God? It's me, Azamat again. I... er. I don't know if you spoke to me just now, but, well, I was wondering if you'd let me ask you something. Will you forgive me? Will you forgive me for being such a loser and making such a mess of my life? I'm sorry I made some really bad choices. I'm sorry for what I did and for what I almost did. Now I'm paying for it, I suppose, but I want to believe that there's more to life than this. If I can only know that you forgive me, then I know I can do better. And you know what, God? Can you help me forgive myself too? I did some pretty stupid things, but I'm not going to let them define me anymore. I want to forgive myself and let go of the past. I'm ready to walk into the future now, with you, if you'll let me. Could you show me how? I'm ready to listen now.

Azamat looked up, not sure what more to say. Was that good enough? Would God answer him again? He did feel lighter, as if a cloud had lifted. He felt better about himself now, and yet there was something more that needed to be done, he just didn't know what that was. At least he'd taken a step in the right direction. He needed to talk to Bela and Michael again, that was for sure.

A chaffinch flew down to the wall and perched just a little distance away from Azamat's shoulder. It cocked its head to one side as if it were studying Azamat intently. Then it gave a little chirp as if it were satisfied and flew away.

Azamat brushed off his jeans and walked back out into the sunshine, a new confidence in his stride. He hadn't got to where he was going yet, but he was on the right path, he knew that now without a doubt.

Chapter 26

Bela

The tram pulled up and Tina jumped on, turning to give a quick wave before she disappeared inside. Bela and Irina waved back and waited until the tram had moved off before continuing their walk across the bridge and towards the park that was situated near both their apartments and not too far from Angelina's school.

"She seems like a lovely girl," said Irina.

"Yes, she is. I'm so glad you got to meet her," Bela answered.

"You've been getting to know her through the Circassian Christian Group?"

"Yes. She has a lot of questions!" Bela laughed. "I keep telling her I don't know all the answers, but I do my best. I think she just needs a friend she can talk to about these things. I understand her family situation back home doesn't exactly warrant free, open discussions about religious matters."

"I'm sure you're doing a great job." Irina linked

her arm through Bela's. "I think it's great that you've got involved in that group. I kind of wish I had something like that I could go to."

"Well, what's stopping you?" Bela asked.

"Um, not being Circassian for one!"

Bela stopped walking for a moment and turned to her friend. "How do you know you're not Circassian? You said you couldn't find your adoption papers. Maybe you are?"

Irina stopped too and sat down on the nearby bench. Bela joined her. "You're right. I've no idea about my parentage. I could be anything. I guess I've always assumed I'm just Russian through and through."

"What does your mother, I mean Lida, what does she say about it?" asked Bela.

"Oh, she's definitely my mother. We might not be blood-related, but she's my mother in all other meanings of the word."

"Yes, I'm sorry. I didn't mean to offend you."

Irina's face softened. "I know, I'm sorry. It can be hard, sometimes, you know. Being adopted. There's always a little part of you that feels lost."

Bela nodded. "I see that in Angelina, sometimes. It's like she's not completely whole. It's like there's something missing."

"Well, I'm glad she knows who her parents were and that she got to be with them if only for a few years. That'll be a great comfort to her when she's older." Irina looked thoughtful.

"Yes, I know. Her parents were lovely." A tear started brimming in Bela's eye and she wiped it away. The pain of losing her best friend in such a tragic way was still quite raw, even after all these years.

Irina gave her a hug. "Now it's my turn to apologise for upsetting you." She let go and turned her gaze to the park beyond them. "To answer your question, my mother says she honestly doesn't know, and I believe her. Apparently, my file was lost. Maybe it was an accident, maybe it was stolen, no one will ever know. That's one of the reasons Mama and Papa adopted me. It would have been hard to find other adoptive parents without a proper file, but Mama was able to push all the paperwork through for herself. She knew the system and the loopholes."

"And they've been good parents? You've been happy?"

Irina's eyes shone. "They've been the best. I'm so lucky. They've loved me like I was their own. There's never even been any favouritism with Daniel. I've heard sometimes that can happen when one child is adopted and the other isn't. It might be unconscious, but it can still be there. I can honestly say I've never felt that they've treated us any differently."

"That's great. They do seem like lovely parents. But..." Should she keep pushing Irina for more information? She just had to know. She had to find a little clue that might link Irina to, well, her real birth mother.

Irina stood up suddenly. "Hey, enough of this melancholy talk. I'm starving and I'm sure Mama's got something wonderful cooking on the stove. Do you want to join us?"

"Thanks, but I'd better not. I need to pick Angelina up from school." Bela checked her watch. "Oh, my goodness, is that the time? I hope I'm not late."

"I'll walk fast with you. I'm sure you'll make it." Irina took off at quite a stride and Bela struggled a little to keep up.

"How's she doing, Angelina? Has she settled into Moscow life?" Irina asked as they exited the park and turned left onto the main road.

"Oh, she's doing really well. She says she loves her new school, and she's made a couple of good friends too. Michael and I are so happy. It was one of my main concerns before we moved here," Bela panted.

"That's great. Children are so resilient."

"Yes, they are," agreed Bela. "Yes, they are."

"Michael, I really think Irina might be my half-sister," Bela blurted out later that evening as soon as Angelina had gone to bed and she and Michael had collapsed onto the sofa in front of the television.

"Woah, hang on a minute. Back up there. What?" Michael put down the television remote and swivelled round towards her, his eyes wide.

"Oh, have I not told you about my suspicions?" Perhaps she had been a little obsessed by all of this over the past few weeks and kept it to herself. It was hard to remember, sometimes, what she had told Michael and what she hadn't.

"This is the first I'm hearing of it, that's for sure." Michael raised an eyebrow. He was used to Bela having these crazy ideas. Insisting on visiting Pavel in the police station. Going round to see Maria. He hadn't been quite so supportive of that idea once she'd told him what she'd done.

"I guess I have a bit of explaining to do," she said sheepishly.

"I think you have," he said, with a smile.

Bela told him about her conversation with Mama back in January. And then about how she'd found out Mama had come to stay with Lida to have the baby.

"Have I really not told you all of this already?" she asked.

"No, it's all new to me. But I guess that might be partly my fault. I've been rather busy setting up things at the office. Perhaps we haven't had much of a chance to talk recently. But carry on, I'm all ears."

Bela filled him in on her conversations with Irina. "It just seems to make so much sense, you know? The timing's about right. The suspicious disappearance of Irina's file. And wouldn't Lida be just the kind of person to look after her own distant relative rather than allow her to grow up in an orphanage?"

Michael thought for a moment. "Yes, I can see how it might all fit. But you don't know anything for sure. Don't go making accusations you might regret later. I think you need to go slowly on this one. It seems like your mother and Lida didn't really want anyone finding out about what had happened. You might start rocking the boat for no particular reason and upsetting a lot of people in the process."

"No particular reason?" Bela's cheeks flushed hot. "I think I have a right to know if I have a half-sister, don't I?"

"I'm not sure, sweetie. All I'm saying is, don't rush into anything. Promise?"

Bela sank back down onto the sofa. "Okay, I promise. But I bet I'm right."

Michael turned back to the television and put his arm around her as he clicked through to one of his favourite shows. Bela pretended to watch too, but her mind was still whirring. What would her next step be? Should she confront Lida? No, she needed more proof. Perhaps she should get some more information from Mama. Yes, that was it. Maybe Mama could be more specific about exactly what had happened. Mama would understand why Bela wanted to know more about her own half-sister. But it wasn't the sort of thing you could talk about over the phone. She might have to be patient. Ugh! That was something that she found so difficult to do. If only she were a bit more laid-back, like Michael.

Chapter 27

Milana

October in Moscow was a lot colder than in Shekala. Milana exited the airport and looked around at the array of taxis and other vehicles. She tightened her coat around her and stuffed her hands into her pockets. Alikhan joined her, dragging both her suitcase and his behind him.

"Shall I get a taxi, Mama?"

"Yes, I've got the address of the hotel somewhere in here." She rummaged around in her purse while Alikhan negotiated a fare with the taxi driver and piled their suitcases into the back of the black Mercedes.

Milana settled herself in the back, while Alikhan sat in the front next to the driver. It had only been eight months since Murat had died, and her son was already taking to his duties as the protective male of the family. It was hard to believe he was still only sixteen. He'd shot up in height over the summer and the beginnings of a small moustache were forming on his upper lip.

Oh, Murat. Where are you when I need you? You were supposed to guide your son through these teenage years, not me. What do I know about teenage boys and all their hormones?

She still thought about Murat a lot, but the pain of losing him had lessened its grip on her heart. She would always be thankful that they'd been reconciled and that she'd told him she loved him before he died. She would be able to move on without regret when the time came. As for Alikhan, he still missed his father terribly, although he wouldn't admit it. The whole experience seemed to have aged him, and she missed his carefree laughter and boyish ways.

They drew up to the entrance of the hotel. The other dancers in the ensemble would be staying here too, but not everyone had been able to afford to come by plane. Milana had decided to come for an extra couple of days to give her a chance to show Alikhan around Moscow a bit. It was his first visit.

She paid the driver, registered them both at the hotel's front desk and found their room on the fifth floor. Alikhan threw himself onto one of the single beds and lay back. For a minute he looked like a little boy again, like the old Alikhan. Milana smiled.

"I can't believe we're here, Mama!"

"Well, you worked hard this year. Of course they'd choose you to be part of the team dancing in the nationals."

"And to think we won the regionals again this summer. That's twice in a row."

Milana tousled his hair and sat on the edge of the other bed. She took off her high heels and wiggled her stockinged feet.

"We'll meet up with Alyona and her mother

tomorrow."

Alikhan nodded. "I hope the coach journey wasn't too bad. I'd hate to be cooped up for so long. She was really dreading it."

Milana was glad that the two were getting on so well. They seemed to have worked out a new way of relating, now that they knew they were cousins. It was great that Alikhan had a proper cousin now. It had always been a regret of hers that both she and Murat had been only children.

"I didn't tell you, Alikhan, but Alyona's uncle is coming too. To see the finals. He wanted to see you both dance. I hope that's okay."

"You've been in contact with him?" Alikhan's tone was almost accusatory. Milana felt herself blushing as if she'd done something wrong.

"Only about this. He rang me to check if it was okay."

"And you didn't ask me?"

"Well, I didn't think I could refuse, since he's coming to see Alyona too. We don't have to see him if you don't want to."

"Will he be coming with us tomorrow?"

"That's your call."

"Okay, I'll think about it."

"Okay."

Milana knew not to push it any further. What would it feel like to see Azamat again? She hadn't seen him since Murat's accident. Azamat had stayed away just like she'd asked, and she was thankful to him for that. But was it time to start where they had left off? Was it time to introduce him into Alikhan's life again? She sighed. Tomorrow might be a difficult and awkward day for everyone.

The next day dawned bright and sunny. There was a crisp chill in the air, a reminder that winter was hard on the heels of autumn, but that just made it perfect sightseeing weather. The leaves had already turned yellow, brown and russet, and the trees here looked barer than the ones down in Shekala. There was something thrilling about being back in the capital. Today she wanted to show Alikhan all the sights, but perhaps she and Madina would have a chance to slip into one of the foreign boutiques and do some shopping.

They ate their breakfast of *kasha*, slices of bread with cheese and *kolbasa*, and black tea with lemon. The hotel dining room was busy, and Milana recognised some of the other Talinka dancers and their parents. Madina and Alyona would be checking in later that morning, and they had planned to meet up in Red Square just after lunch.

"I thought we'd spend the morning in Ismailovsky Park, what do you think?" she asked Alikhan.

"Is that where all the souvenirs are? Sounds good. I promised Nana and Granddad I'd bring them back something," he said. Murat's parents had asked her for some particular items too, so she needed to look out for those.

"I'm sure you'll find something they'll like."

They had a lot of fun riding the metro and then browsing around all the stalls. Alikhan chose a patterned tea towel set for Nana and a decorative vodka glass for his granddad. He also bought some sweets and chocolates that looked a little different to the ones they were used to in Shekala.

From Ismailovsky Park, they headed back into the

centre. Milana had promised to take Alikhan to
McDonald's. She'd only been once herself, so she was
just as excited as he was. A café in Shekala had tried to
replicate the famous American fast-food chain, but it
wasn't the same.

They exited the metro at Pushkinskaya and
walked across toward the golden arches. Alikhan was so
excited he was practically jumping up and down. There
were a lot of tourists milling around this area too. Why
would you come all the way to Russia only to eat at
McDonald's? But then, it was probably familiar and safe.
Even the names of the meals were basically in English
with Russian letters. She read them out. 'Big Mac'. 'Fillet
o' Fish'. Murat would have found this so funny. What a
shame he couldn't be here to enjoy this with them.

Their stomachs full, they jumped back on the
metro to Okhotny Ryad, and walked back out into the
sunshine along with the myriad of tourists from all over
the world.

"There they are!" Alikhan called, as he spotted
Alyona in the crowd just inside the entrance to Red
Square. He waved wildly, and Alyona waved back.
Milana ran to give her friend a hug.

"I'm so glad you made it. How was the journey?"
she asked Madina.

"Oh, not too bad. We had a rest in the hotel room
before we came out here, but I may fall asleep at any
minute. I don't think I slept a wink on that bus." Madina
did look tired, but there was a certain sparkle in her eyes.
"We've brought someone else with us," she added.

Milana looked over to where Madina was
indicating, and saw a familiar figure hanging back,
slightly unsure of when to come forward to be
introduced.

Milana took the initiative. "Oleg, I believe. How

nice to meet you properly, at last."

Oleg shook her hand and then held his arm out for Madina, who shyly linked her arm through his. Milana gave her friend a look which she hoped conveyed 'We'll talk about this later; I want to hear all about it!'.

The five of them had a wonderful afternoon, wandering around the Kremlin, queueing up to take a look inside Lenin's mausoleum, and admiring the beautiful architecture of St Basil's cathedral. They wandered through the iconic shopping centre, GUM, and then settled down for a cup of coffee in a nearby café.

"Oh, my feet are killing me already," Milana groaned, removing her shoes briefly to rub her aching soles. "I don't know why I didn't wear more sensible shoes."

"It's because you always look so glamorous," smiled Madina. "It's the price you pay."

"I suppose you're right. But now…," Milana glanced around to check that Oleg, who had gone to order their drinks, was out of earshot. "You've got to tell me what *he's* doing here. I want to know everything!"

Madina laughed. She seemed so happy in that moment that Milana didn't think she'd ever seen her friend look more beautiful. "He asked to come. I told him all about Alyona's dance troupe, and he insisted on taking time off work to join us."

"Oh?" Milana raised a suggestive eyebrow.

"Oh no," Madina shook her head, "It's nothing like that. He's being very gentlemanly. Separate rooms and all that. But it is nice to have some time together, the three of us."

"Is Alyona okay with it?" Milana lowered her voice, but Alyona and Alikhan were deep in their own conversation and clearly weren't paying any attention to what their mothers were talking about.

"Yes, she seems to really like him. I'm so glad."

"And, Musa. Does he know?"

Madina's eyes narrowed in disapproval. "I told him about the dance competition, but he found some excuse not to come. Ever since I turned him down, he seems to have lost interest in Alyona too. I know I made the right decision, but I'm sad for her. It seems he didn't really want to be a good father after all. I should have known that a leopard doesn't change its spots."

Oleg came back to the table, and Madina sat back, the smile returning to her face. "But did I tell you that Mama came up too?"

"Your mother, really?"

"Yes. She flew up with Azamat. Papa couldn't make it, of course, but Mama was quite excited once Azamat talked her into it. I don't think she's left Shekala for years."

"Oh, that's wonderful." Milana swallowed a lump in her throat. She'd been prepared to bump into Azamat tomorrow at the competition, but not his mother. Why that should be a problem, she wasn't sure. But all those years ago, when they'd been together, she'd never once met his parents. It seemed a bit strange to be doing it now. Did Azamat's mother know about Alikhan? Madina wouldn't have mentioned it, would she? She would have to ask her later. Oh dear, this could be awkward.

Chapter 28

Azamat

The evening had been spectacular. Azamat hadn't realised quite how much he would enjoy himself watching all the dances. It had transported him back to the time when he'd been dancing in a similar troupe himself. Would he ever have got as good as this if he'd stuck it out? Maybe. But it was too late for regrets. To be able to watch his niece and his own son performing to the best of their ability had been reward enough.

Azamat guided his mother out of the auditorium into the corridor. It had taken a lot of persuading to get her to come, but she'd clearly enjoyed it. Her eyes were glowing with pride, giving her a youthful look that he hadn't seen since Papa got shot.

"Hey, Nana, Uncle Azamat, what did you think?"

Alyona came running up to them in the corridor, the buzz of adrenaline clearly still coursing through her body so that she was practically skipping with joy like a little girl again. Azamat gave her a big hug.

"You were amazing. Perfect. I couldn't take my eyes off you."

"And second place overall!"

"That's a brilliant result. Everyone must be so proud."

"Yeah, we're having a big party later, back at the hotel."

Azamat's attention moved to just behind Alyona, where Madina and her friend Oleg were walking towards them. The two of them were busy chatting to Milana and Alikhan. Alyona must have sensed his distraction, for she turned around.

"Hey, Alikhan!" she said, looking first at her friend and then back at her uncle.

"Hey," Alikhan replied.

Alikhan's eyes met Azamat's. The look they gave him wasn't aggressive, to Azamat's relief, but it seemed to convey the message that he didn't want to talk to him and didn't want him to come any closer. Azamat took the hint and stayed where he was, next to Mama, who was busy fussing over Alyona. He nodded to Madina and then rested his gaze on Milana. She still took his breath away. He felt like a nervous teenager again as she approached him.

"I'm sorry we weren't able to meet up yesterday."

"That's okay, I understand. Mama and I had a lovely day doing our own thing."

Milana glanced back at Alikhan. "He, er, just wasn't ready. I'm sorry."

"It's okay, really. I heard you had a good time."

He hoped the lightness in his voice covered up his true feelings. He had been very disappointed to learn that Alikhan didn't want him to come on the sightseeing trip. He'd spent a reasonably happy day with Mama, but he'd been constantly wondering what everyone else was doing. But he couldn't hold that against the boy. Perhaps things would have been different if they'd had the chance to get to know each other before Murat had died. Again, it was too late for regrets. He had to give the boy space, he had to respect his feelings. An image of Pavel's angry face flashed into his mind once more and he shook his head to get rid of it. No, he was going to do everything he could to make sure that his son had no reason to hate him.

Milana was telling him all about their day, but he'd heard the whole story from Alyona and Madina already.

"It was just so much fun. I feel so alive in a big city like this. The shops were amazing."

"I heard you nearly bought them all out."

Milana laughed, and the sound tinkled like music in his ears. When was the last time he'd properly heard her laugh?

"Not quite, but let's just say we'll be on starvation rations for the next month or two."

Milana glanced at Mama a couple of times, but Mama was pretending not to notice her. Azamat was grateful that Mama had understood his need to keep his connection with Milana and her son away from public scrutiny for the time being.

Milana, looking a little relieved, lowered her voice and placed her hand on his arm. "Do you want me to talk to him again?"

Azamat saw a flicker of annoyance run across Alikhan's face as he saw what Milana had done, and he gently removed his arm.

"No, no it's okay. I don't think he's ready, and I don't want to push him."

"Okay. Maybe in a few months. When the time is right."

"Yes. You'll let me know?"

"Yes, of course."

"So, you're heading back home tomorrow?"

"Yes." Milana's smile was back. "We have a morning flight. You?"

"Mama and I are spending a couple of days with my other sister, Bela, and her husband, and then flying back on Wednesday."

"Oh, that will be lovely. Well, it was good to see you again, Azamat."

"You too, Milana."

She walked away from him, as she had done so many times before in his life. It didn't take much to open up old wounds of pain, he observed. His heart had never properly healed from losing Milana. Perhaps it never would. But pursuing her now might be the thing that would drive Alikhan away from him, and he could never risk that. Never.

It was good to spend time with his younger sister again. He hadn't realised quite how much he'd been missing Bela, Michael and Angelina until now. There was something about their little family of three that made him yearn to be part of it. He couldn't quite put his finger on what it was. Was it the way they treated each other? The atmosphere in their apartment? He felt at peace in their home, and Mama also seemed less anxious and, well, happier.

It was the day after the competition. Milana and Alikhan had flown home. Madina and Alyona were on the long bus journey back, together with Madina's friend, Oleg, and the rest of them were at this moment taking a walk around the park nearest to Bela and Michael's apartment.

He seemed alright, that Oleg guy. They'd got to chat a little over dinner after the dance competition, when the whole family had got together. Azamat felt some responsibility towards his sister to make sure she was treated with respect. Ever since she'd divorced that idiot, Musa, that is. Now that she and Alyona were back under the roof of her parents' home it was his job to look after them. His and Papa's, of course, although Papa worked such long hours he was barely around. No, Oleg had kept his sister's honour intact and Azamat had warmed to his friendly, laid-back personality very quickly. It was good to see that Madina was moving on with her life. It was good for Alyona, too. She deserved only the best.

"A penny for your thoughts?" Michael had hung back to chat with him.

"Sorry?"

"It's an English expression. You seem deep in thought about something, that's all," Michael said.

"I was thinking about Madina's new acquaintance, Oleg, that's all. He seems alright, don't you think?" It might be good to get Michael's opinion. Azamat trusted his judgement.

"Oh, I only got to meet him very briefly at dinner, but yes, I liked him a lot. I think he would be good for Madina, and Alyona seems to like him a lot too. I'm happy she's found someone like him."

"I'm glad you think so too." Azamat studied the family group ahead of them. Angelina was skipping around, clearly very excited by all the visitors, and eager to show them around her new home here in Moscow.

"And how are you doing, Azamat?" Michael asked in that serious, probing tone of his that meant that they were about to have a deep talk about something. Azamat was about to brush off the question with a quick reply, but maybe it would be a good opportunity to go deeper, like Michael wanted.

"It's okay, actually. I, er, I've been talking to God a little bit. Asking for forgiveness, that is."

"Oh, that's great. And how does that make you feel? Has anything changed?" Michael's pace slowed, and Azamat slowed too, turning to face him. He thrust his hands in his pockets and looked at the ground.

"Good, I think. I feel like I can live in the present now, instead of allowing the past to haunt me. I guess I'm feeling more optimistic about the future." He paused. Why was it so hard to talk about these things?

"Do you believe God has forgiven you?" Michael asked.

"Yes, yes I think so," said Azamat, looking Michael in the eye again. "Although I feel like there's a final step I'm missing out on somewhere."

"And have you forgiven yourself?" said Michael.

"I'm working on it."

Michael started walking again. The rest of the family had already reached the end of the path and were waiting for them. "I'd love to talk to you more about that this evening, if that's okay. I've got a great book I think you'd like," he said.

Azamat nodded. "Sure, that would be good."

Back at the apartment Bela and Mama had put together quite a feast for dinner. The conversation had turned back to the dance competition.

"I was so proud of Alyona," Mama was saying. "She looked so beautiful, so graceful. It's such a shame you had to miss it, Bela."

"I know Mama, but it couldn't be helped. I'm sure it was wonderful," Bela replied.

Mama narrowed her eyes a little and looked at Azamat. "And that Alikhan boy, he was rather good too."

Azamat shifted in his chair. Everyone in the room now knew that Alikhan was his son. Alyona hadn't been able to keep that secret for very long, and it was easier now that the secret was out in the open. Mama was desperate to get to know this long-lost grandson of hers, but Azamat had persuaded her to keep her distance. He knew she was finding it hard, but it was killing him even more.

"Mama," he said, his voice low, his eyebrows raised.

"I know, I know. I was just saying," she protested.

"Mama, will you help me with the dishes?" Bela asked suddenly, getting up out of her seat and collecting a handful of dirty plates.

Azamat exhaled slowly. He and Michael turned to the subject of Michael's linguistic work, until eventually Michael declared that it was time for Angelina to go to bed. Michael excused himself, and Azamat picked up a couple of plates of biscuits and sweets to return them to the kitchen. He reached the door, but then held back instinctively. Mama and Bela's voices were low and hushed. They were talking about something important. Were they talking about Alikhan?

"Mama, please tell me a little more. I'm desperate to know." Bela's soft-spoken voice carried over the sound of dishes clinking in the sink.

"It's all in the past now, there's no point," said Mama.

"But what if it's not, Mama?"

"What do you mean?"

The clinking of dishes stopped and the sound of water flowing from the tap ceased. Bela continued. "I know about Lida, Mama. I know that you came here all those years ago to have the baby."

"Lida had no right to tell you," came Mama's

sharp retort.

"She didn't. I just figured it out myself. And I think I know what happened to your baby."

"You do?" Mama's voice was full of surprise. Azamat inhaled sharply and nearly dropped the plates he was carrying.

"Yes. I think I know who my half-sister is." Bela's voice was quivering. Azamat's mind was racing. A half-sister? Another sibling they hadn't known about? What was going on?

There was a pause. "I don't think you do, *lapochka*." Mama's voice was steady now.

"Why not?"

"Because the baby I gave birth to was definitely a little boy."

Chapter 29

Bela

Bela reeled backwards like she'd been hit in the stomach. What? A boy? Not a girl? Then, Irina couldn't be her long-lost sister after all. She collapsed onto the nearest stool.

"But… But it all made sense. It all fit together."

"What did, *lapochka*?" Her mother sat down next to her.

"How you had gone to stay with Lida to have the baby. And how Lida and Vladimir had adopted the baby to make sure that it went to a good home and didn't grow up in the orphanage."

"I'm sorry, but it sounds like you've got it all wrong. Lida must have put the baby in the orphanage after all."

"But there were no records. Irina's birth records are lost."

"Things like that just happen, *lapochka*. It was just a coincidence, that's all." Mama's voice was soothing as she stroked Bela's hand.

"I'm sorry, Mama, I shouldn't have brought it up. I obviously jumped to the wrong conclusion."

"It's okay, no harm done," replied Mama. "Well," she continued, her voice stern, "other than the fact that Azamat has been listening at the door the whole time, and now I have to explain to him about the other step-brother he never knew about."

Azamat appeared around the corner of the doorframe holding two plates of biscuits and looking sheepish.

"Oops. I'll leave you to it, then," said Bela, quickly hurrying off towards the living room. She'd made a mess of things again and didn't want to deal with Mama's anger right now.

She found Michael and explained what had happened.

"I feel so stupid, I should have listened to you before I went racing ahead with my own theories," she admitted.

"Don't worry, it's okay." He gave her a hug.

"All those months I've been getting to know Irina, thinking she was my sister. She must have thought it was really weird, the way I kept hanging around her."

"I'm sure she was just glad to have found a new friend. And there's no reason you can't be friends. You're still technically distant cousins."

"I know. But it still hasn't solved the question of what happened to Mama's baby. I'm back to square one. There are no records. It seems like the child just vanished into thin air."

It wasn't quite the reunion she had been anticipating. Lida had invited them all over for dinner the evening before Mama and Azamat were due to fly home. Bela had built up in her mind a tearful reunion between Mama and Irina, with hugs all round, and the secret finally out in the open. But that wasn't going to happen now. In fact, it might be rather awkward. Now that Azamat knew about Mama's baby, there would be a lot of unanswered questions hanging in the air, and Mama was clearly angry that now Azamat knew her secret too. At least Lida had no idea of any of this. What a relief Bela had never voiced her suspicions. Perhaps they could all pretend that there was nothing going on and that everything was as it always was. Mama and Azamat were simply visiting a long-lost cousin, that was all.

The evening was perfectly pleasant. Mama and Lida had hugged and renewed their old friendship. They chatted together happily about all the years since they'd last met. Bela kept looking anxiously from one to another, but neither side was letting on that there had been any secret that needed to be hidden.

"I'm sorry you weren't able to meet my eldest daughter, Madina, and my granddaughter, Alyona," Mama was saying, in between forkfuls of Lida's delicious fish and *smetana* salad.

"Oh, that's okay. I'm sure we'll meet again some time. I heard they did marvellously. Second place wasn't it?" said Lida.

"Yes, second place. A real honour." Mama's eyes shone with pride.

Daniel hadn't been able to make it that evening, for some reason, but Mama, Lida, Vladimir and Irina chatted away happily without any awkwardness at all. How silly Bela had been to think that Irina was her long-lost sister. When was she going to learn to stop jumping to conclusions?

Finally, it was time to leave. Everyone said their goodbyes, and Lida promised to make a visit down to Shekala one day.

"I haven't been back to my homeland for years. I would like to see the place again," she said, her eyes soft with memories and regrets.

"You and Vladimir would be most welcome," Mama replied, and Bela could tell she genuinely meant it and wasn't just being polite.

Just then, a key turned in the lock and the front door opened. It was Daniel.

"I'm so sorry, I've only just got back from work. Am I too late to meet the guests?" he said. He turned to Azamat and shook hands. "You must be Azamat. It's great to meet you."

Azamat clasped both hands around Daniel's. "You too."

Then Daniel turned to Mama, who was standing just behind Azamat.

"And you must be cousin Radima," he said.

Mama froze for a moment. A strange look had come over her face, like she'd seen a ghost. It was just for a second, and she recovered quickly, but Bela had noticed it. A quick look at Lida showed that she, too, had frozen for a second. Her eyes were wide and her face suddenly pale. What was going on? Lida had obviously not expected Daniel to come back in time to meet Mama and Azamat, but why was she so nervous about them meeting?

Bela's mind started whirring again. Could it be? But how?

Chapter 30

Bela

Four weeks had passed since the dinner party at Lida's house. Four, painful weeks. Bela had been ready to let go the idea of having found her half-sister and had accepted that it was back to the drawing board. But now? What was that strange look that had passed over Mama's face when Daniel had walked in? And why had Lida looked so nervous and worried?

It wasn't possible that Daniel was her long-lost brother, was it? Both Lida and Irina had been adamant that Daniel hadn't been adopted.

Bela was back in Lida's living room, waiting for Lida to get ready for the Circassian Christian meeting. They were due to travel together since the evenings were so dark now in late November. Lida was taking her time as usual, giving Bela a chance to sit and think. She walked over to the bookcase where there were a number of family photos on display. What was it Irina had said? There were lots of photos of Daniel as a baby, but none of her until she was adopted at around six months old.

Bela picked up a photo of a little baby, lying on a blanket. She guessed that the baby was about a month old, so it must be of Daniel. But could Daniel be Mama's baby? Lida would have put him in the orphanage, like Mama had asked. Even if she had adopted him later, it took months for the paperwork to go through. Bela knew that better than anyone, now that she'd worked in the orphanage office for several months.

She fingered the edge of the photo frame. It was a little loose on one side, so she turned it over to fasten it back into place. But as she did so, she noticed something sticking out from underneath the black cardboard backing. A piece of paper? She worked the clasps loose and removed the back of the frame completely. Yes, it was a piece of paper. She shouldn't be snooping, but she couldn't help it. Carefully, slowly, she opened up the piece of paper.

"Bela?"

Bela spun around, her cheeks glowing hot suddenly. She'd been caught doing something she shouldn't have. But there was no time to put the paper back. No time to come up with a reasonable explanation. She just stood there, the photo frame in one hand and the piece of paper in the other.

"Bela?" Lida asked again, her face white.

"I'm sorry, Lida, but I have to know. I didn't mean to pry, but this kind of … well…."

Lida stepped forward to take the piece of paper, but Bela took a step back. "Is this what I think it is?"

"Bela, please!" Lida's eyes were wide and pleading.

"This wouldn't happen to be Daniel's birth certificate, would it?" Bela couldn't stop herself. She'd spent months searching for this document, and here it was in her hands at last.

Lida slumped into the chair nearest her. "Yes," she said weakly.

"And, is it possible that I might find my mother's name on it too?"

Lida nodded. A rush of remorse suddenly came over Bela. What was she doing? She loved this woman almost as much as she loved her own mother. She knelt at Lida's feet. "I'm so sorry, Lida. I didn't mean to find out this way. I didn't mean to hurt you."

Lida gave a long sigh and looked straight into Bela's eyes. "I think I have some explaining to do. I think we'd better give the Circassian group a miss tonight."

There was a long silence. Bela was still in shock, her mind aching with the enormity of what she'd just discovered.

"I think it's probably time I told you the rest of the story," said Lida at last.

Bela nodded, unable to speak. She settled herself in one of the other chairs, her hands still clasping the unopened piece of paper.

"My husband, Vladimir, and I were very deeply in love," Lida began. "We still are of course. But the one sadness in our life was that we couldn't seem to have children. We'd actually started talking about adopting one of the children at the orphanage, but it's always complicated, you see. I didn't want to get into trouble for mixing my professional life with my personal life."

"And then my mother rang you out of the blue."

"Yes, yes she did. I promise you that the idea of us adopting her baby didn't come to my mind until she was almost about to deliver. I guess I was hoping she'd decide to keep the baby. I see so many unhappy, abandoned children at the orphanage. I would have done anything to save her baby from feeling that too."

Bela nodded, thinking of Angelina and the day

she'd collected her from the orphanage in Beslan.

"Anyway, your mother was determined not to keep the baby. I think she was hurting deep inside, but she was proud. She wanted your father more, and if giving up the baby was the price she had to pay, then that's what she was going to do. Please don't feel badly about her, Bela. That was just the way of things back then. We didn't have the kind of choices that you young people have today."

"I think Mama has already paid for her choices many times over," said Bela sadly.

Lida continued. "The baby came a couple of weeks early and we didn't have a bed ready in the orphanage for a newborn, so I handed him to a friend to look after for a few days. She was a nurse who worked for us at the orphanage. I knew she'd take good care of him, but I knew we couldn't keep him with us until your mother had left. I thought she would stay with us another month, you know, to recover properly, but it seems she just wanted to run back home and forget this had ever happened. I tried to stop her, but she insisted on going back to Shekala about a week after the baby was born. She was miserable, and she no longer had a reason to be here.

Anyway, I went to collect the baby from my nurse friend and agreed to look after him at our home for a while. He was a little colicky, and we weren't sure he was ready to join the others at the orphanage just yet."

"And that's when you decided to keep him?"

"Yes. We fell in love with him, Vladimir and I. And it all made so much sense. This baby was related to me. I felt a duty to make sure he had a good life."

"What did you tell the orphanage?"

"We said a family had been found for him. It wasn't a lie. I just never told anyone that we were that family."

"And that's why there's no file on him at the orphanage."

"Yes. He never went there, you see. He was never officially adopted. We arranged all the paperwork ourselves. I feel a bit bad about that, hiding his real birth certificate and fabricating a new one that had my name and Vladimir's on it. But I honestly thought we were doing what was best, please believe me."

"Did you ever tell my mother?"

"I tried to contact her once or twice, but I couldn't get through. And then time just slipped by. I promised myself I would tell her if she ever called or visited again, but she never did. And then we kind of forgot. It was so wonderful to have a son. We were so happy."

A tear slipped down Lida's cheek, and Bela squeezed her hand sympathetically.

"It's okay, I think you did the right thing."

"You do? You're not angry on behalf of your mother?"

"No, I'm not angry. I'm just so excited that I've found my half-brother at last, and that he should be Daniel, whom I already love like a brother. That's just God at work in a wonderful way, don't you think?"

Lida smiled and wiped away a tear. "Yes, He does work in wonderful ways."

"Does Daniel know?"

"No. Irina knows that she's adopted, but he doesn't."

"Oh, okay. So, I can't tell him I'm his half-sister?"

"Please don't, not just yet. Give us time. We'll tell him the news ourselves and then let you know, is that okay?"

"Yes, of course. I understand. Wow! This has all

been a lot to process!" Bela leaned back against the chair. It was so good to have solved the mystery of Mama's baby and the missing adoption records. And that it should be Daniel!

"Will you tell your mother?" Lida asked, a little anxiously.

"I don't know. I'll pray about it. Let's talk again sometime soon. I'm glad the mystery is finally solved, but I need to sort it all out in my head, first.

"I admit, I do feel relieved that you found out," said Lida. "I so wanted to tell you, and that moment that your mother and Daniel came face to face, I thought my heart was about to stop beating."

"Yes, I noticed. That's when I became suspicious," said Bela. "But why do you think Mama reacted so strangely? She's never met Daniel before, and she had no idea you'd adopted him."

"I suppose, now that he's all grown up, he might look a little like his real father, and perhaps she recognised him," Lida suggested.

"Yes, you must be right. So maybe Mama knows? Maybe she's worked it out too?"

"I guess it's possible," said Lida.

"Oh, my goodness, there's so much to think about. But do you know, I'm so happy that it worked out like this. It means that we have even more in common now." Bela got up and gave Lida a big hug. This long-lost family of hers was becoming more and more special. God was so good.

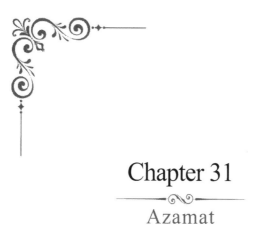

Chapter 31

Azamat

It was certainly freezing outside. About minus ten, at a guess. Azamat quickly locked up the shop and rubbed his gloved hands together as he walked briskly over to where he'd parked his car. He hadn't been expecting the call from Alyona. She and Alikhan had apparently been stranded after dance practice when their marshroutka had broken down. Azamat could only imagine the conversation that had gone on between the two teens before Alyona had been allowed to phone her uncle to come and pick them up. It was almost a year since Murat had died and still there had been no meaningful contact between him and his son. Yes, they'd seen each other in Moscow last October, but the boy hadn't wanted to go near him. Azamat had almost given up hope of ever seeing him again.

He soon found them, on the corner where they'd been stranded, stamping their feet in the snow to keep warm. Alyona waved a hand as she saw Azamat's car approaching. He drew up alongside them and waited for them to bundle themselves in the back.

"If you'd been any longer, Alikhan would have turned into an icicle," Alyona said, laughing. "I mean, look at what he's wearing, the idiot."

"It's alright for you, snug in all your winter gear. How was I to know it was going to snow?" said Alikhan, grumpily.

"It is January, Alikhan, it's not unusual you know?"

Alyona was teasing him, but Alikhan clearly wasn't in the mood.

Azamat turned the heater up to full blast. He turned around and gave Alikhan a smile. "Hi. You alright?" He hoped the boy couldn't see the sadness and the longing in his biological father's face. That he couldn't see how desperately Azamat wanted things to work out between them.

Alikhan paused, and then smiled back. His smile seemed a little shy but genuine.

"Thanks so much for getting us."

"No problem." Azamat turned back round to face the front. "Now, where am I taking you?"

"I think we need to warm up with a hot chocolate at The Orange Café. That's if you've got time, Uncle Azamat?" said Alyona.

"Sure, I've got time for that, if that's what you want," replied Azamat. They both looked earnestly at Alikhan.

There was a slight break in Alikhan's voice when he answered. "Sure, I've nothing important to do."

Azamat wasn't sure what had turned Alikhan around that evening he'd collected the two of them from the *marshroutka* stop, but probably Alyona had given him a talking to. She could be quite direct when she wanted to be, his niece, and he loved that part of her. Maybe time had been a factor too. Alikhan had been grieving for Murat for a long time, but it finally seemed like he was ready to move on. The awkwardness in the café that night had soon evaporated, and they'd all joked around like they were old friends. It had been a miracle. Truly, a mountain had been moved. Since then, Alikhan had been willing to meet up again and things were slowly moving forward.

Thank you, God!

"Got you!" Azamat shouted, as a perfectly formed snowball landed on Alikhan's back.

"You'll pay for that!" laughed Alikhan as he took aim. The snowball came fast, and Azamat had no time to duck before it had hit him square in the face.

"Ow." The snow stung his cheeks and he wiped it out of his eyes. Alikhan jogged over.

"I didn't hurt you, did I?"

"No, just a bit of a shock. I'll get over it." Azamat waited until Alikhan got near enough and then shoved a handful of snow down his back.

"Hey!"

Azamat grinned. This was it. This was what he'd always imagined being a father would be like. He couldn't believe he'd been given a chance to start over again. Yes, he'd missed out on sixteen years already, but he was part of Alikhan's life now, and things were just getting better and better.

"You ready to call it quits and head home?"

"Yes, I'd better. It's school tomorrow."

"Sure, I'll take you back to the village."

"No, it's okay. I can catch a *marshroutka*."

"No, really. I want to. I...er... I enjoy the extra time to chat with you."

Alikhan nodded, and the two of them brushed the snow off their clothes and headed over to where Azamat had parked.

"How's your mother?" asked Azamat, once they were on the road.

"She's okay."

Azamat nodded. He wouldn't press further, although he would have loved to know more about Milana and what she was doing. He missed her. They'd hadn't met since that time in Moscow.

"What happened between you two, anyway?" asked Alikhan.

"What do you mean?"

"Before I was born. Before Mama and Papa got married."

"She hasn't told you?"

"Not really."

"Well, in that case, you should probably ask her to tell her side of the story."

"I want to hear your side," said Alikhan, earnestly.

Azamat gripped the steering wheel a little tighter, as he allowed his mind to go back to that painful time in his past.

"I loved her very much, your mother. We danced together, you know. Like you, in an ensemble. But then we met up again when we were a bit older. I couldn't imagine being with anyone else. But, well, we were young. We got a bit carried away."

"You mean, she got pregnant. With me."

"Yes."

"And you weren't ready to be a father."

"No! I mean, yes!" Azamat stared at Alikhan, his

eyes questioning. "Is that what you think? That I left because I wasn't ready to be a father?"

"Well, wasn't it?"

"No. No, it wasn't like that. It was a shock, of course, but I wanted to do the right thing. I wanted to marry your mother and be a good father. That's what I wanted."

"Oh? I thought... Then why didn't you?"

"I'm afraid your grandparents, your mother's parents that is, didn't think I was good enough for her."

"Why?"

"Well, I didn't always have my life together, like I do now. I didn't have a proper job at the time, I'd dropped out of college. I had no prospects. Besides, I wasn't from the right family line."

"And my father was."

"Yes. Your mother was intended for Murat, since they were little. The pregnancy just speeded things up. When I next saw your mother, she was already engaged."

Azamat swallowed the lump in his throat.

"And you walked away." Alikhan turned his face to the window. Azamat glanced at his son. So many misunderstandings, so much buried anger. No, maybe anger was too strong a word. Disappointment. He hated to think that his son was disappointed with him, but then he'd been disappointed with himself too.

"Alikhan, you have to understand that I had no choice. I walked away, but only because your mother asked me to. She told me it was for the best if I did, if I had nothing to do with her or the baby. She thought it was better for you that I wasn't in your life. I should have fought for you, I know that now. That's my biggest regret. I never was very good at standing up for myself. At doing the right thing. I used to let people walk over me, tell me what to do, you know?"

"But you're different now?"

"Yes, I think so. Something happened to change all that. I'll tell you about it another time. But basically, I found out where that path was going to lead me, and it was a terrible place."

"Why didn't you come and find me sooner?"

Azamat thought a while. "I guess, I didn't think I deserved to be happy again. I didn't deserve to be a father. I'd made some pretty bad choices in life and I needed to forgive myself first."

"And have you done that?"

"Yes, yes I have. What's more, I know that God has forgiven me too. And now I have you back in my life, and I'm never going to take that for granted. I know I'll never replace your other father, but I hope that, in time, we might have something special between us."

Alikhan nodded. "I'd like that."

"We're here." Azamat pulled the car up just outside Milana's home. He turned off the engine and looked at Alikhan, who was still deep in thought.

"I'm glad Alyona told me to give you another chance," he said. Azamat smiled, and Alikhan continued, "But I'm just not ready to call you 'Papa' yet."

"Of course, I understand."

"And, I'm just not ready to have you and my mother... you know... get back together?"

Azamat felt a jolt of pain in his heart, but he swallowed, took a deep breath and looked intently at the young boy next to him, the one that looked so much like him when he was that age.

"Alikhan, I don't know what the future holds for me and your mother. But I do know that neither of us would want to jump into anything if you weren't ready, okay?"

"Okay."

They shook hands and Alikhan got out of the car. He raised his hand in a quick wave and then disappeared inside the family gate.

Azamat sat there for a moment or two. Then he started the engine and slowly rolled away, back down the road towards Shekala.

Chapter 32

Bela

Bela glanced at her phone to check the time. The plane had landed more or less on time, and it had been a smooth flight down from Moscow. As they taxied around the edge of the runway, she could see Mama, Azamat and Alyona waiting for them at the fence, along with all the other families of the passengers on board. She waved, even though they wouldn't be able to see her. Smiling at Angelina, she squeezed her knee.

"It's good to be home, isn't it?"

"How long are we staying, *Tyotya* Bela?" asked Angelina, wide-eyed. Both of them were still so unused to flying that the whole experience was magical, albeit a little nerve-racking at times.

"A whole week. *Tyotya* Madina's wedding is the day after tomorrow. Are you excited?"

"I love going to weddings. I can't wait!" replied Angelina.

It had been well over a year since Bela had left her hometown, the longest she'd ever been away. As she stepped off the plane and onto the tarmac, she paused, took a deep breath and expelled the air slowly. Mountain air!

In a few minutes she'd be reunited with her family, but she felt a slight fluttering in the depths of her stomach. Nerves. She had something huge she had to tell Mama, and she was going to have to find the right time. How would Mama react? It was hard to tell.

Lida and Vladimir had broken the news to Daniel several weeks ago, shortly after the conversation in the kitchen about the discovered birth certificate. Apparently, Daniel had taken it well, once he'd got over the initial shock.

"You're not angry?" Bela had asked him after he'd given her a huge bear hug that left her struggling for breath.

"No, of course not," he'd replied. "It's been a lot to take in, naturally, but I think maybe deep down I knew that something wasn't quite as it should be. I've always felt a little different to my parents, and I could never figure out why until now. And Irina and I have even more in common now, so that's great. No, how could I be angry? God had everything under His control the whole time. He placed me in a wonderful family, and I get to find out that you're actually my half-sister and not just a distant cousin after all."

"I hope we're not a disappointment to you," Bela said, with a little laugh.

"Absolutely not! I know enough about the backgrounds of the children at mother's orphanage to know that my real family could have been a lot more dysfunctional."

Bela grinned. "Well, that's because you haven't got to know everything about us yet. We have our fair share of skeletons in our closets."

"And I'm looking forward to finding out all about them," Daniel teased back.

Bela, Daniel and Lida had discussed the best way to break the news to Mama. They had decided that it would be better coming from Bela, rather than Daniel phoning up out of the blue. Then, while Bela had been considering whether she should fly home or get Mama to fly up to Moscow again, Madina had announced that her wedding would be in the spring. Everyone agreed that it would be best for Bela to break the news after the wedding, once things had calmed down, and that would give Mama some time to think about whether she wanted to meet Daniel again, and if so when.

Well, at least there was the wedding to look forward to first. Bela, Michael and Angelina exited through the large airport doors and found Mama and the others waiting eagerly for them. Mama caught sight of her and soon they were giving each other a fierce hug.

"Mama, it's so good to see you!"

"I've missed you so much, *lapochka*. But you look well."

"I am well, Mama." Bela grinned.

"Oh?"

"No, no, it's nothing like that."

Mama's smile dropped a little bit. She'd obviously been hoping Bela was going to tell her she was pregnant again. At least they'd got that awkward conversation out of the way early on.

"Papa's sorry he couldn't be here, but he'll be home as early as he can tonight. And Madina's had to finish things off at work," said Mama, as she wrapped her arms around Angelina, picking her up off the floor in an enthusiastic embrace. "You've grown so much since October." Angelina grinned. It was true, she'd had a bit of a growth spurt and Bela had had to replace most of her clothes in the last month or two. She couldn't believe her daughter was nearly thirteen.

Michael hugged everyone too and then wheeled both suitcases down towards where Azamat had parked the car. They all squeezed in, with Angelina perched on Bela's lap. Bela couldn't tear her eyes away from the window as the car sped past all the familiar streets and houses. As the car left Shekala on its way to the village of Awush, the buildings thinned out and Bela could at last see the snow-capped, jagged peaks of the mountains in the distance, just beyond the rolling, green foothills. She felt her shoulders relax and her breath deepen.

Yes, it was good to be home.

April weather could be so unpredictable, but the sky outside was blue with just a few white clouds decorating the horizon when Bela pulled back the curtains on the day of the wedding. She rushed into Madina's room, but her sister was already up.

"Can you believe it? For a second time in my life I'm about to leave my childhood home and get married!" said Madina, her eyes sparkling with anticipation.

"I think it's going to be different this time, though," said Bela, squeezing her sister's hand. "The Madina from eighteen years ago was a little young and naïve, if I remember, rushing into a marriage straight out of school."

"I know. I think I hoped it would bring meaning and security to my life. Ha! What a joke. I would do anything to turn back time and give my younger self a good talking to. What a waste all those years were. Well, apart from Alyona of course. Being Alyona's mother has been the best thing that ever happened to me."

"But now you've been given a second chance. How many people are that lucky?"

"I know. I'm so happy, Bela, I think I'm going to burst!"

"Are you awake, Mama?" Alyona's voice called through the door.

"Yes, of course, sweetie, come in."

Alyona entered, a towel wrapped around her head and another one around her body. "You need to get going, both of you, come on. The bathroom's free."

"You go first," said Bela to Madina. "You've got a lot more to get ready than I have."

Madina grabbed her bath robe and gave her daughter a hug as she passed her at the door. Bela smiled at Alyona as she hurried back to her own room to prepare for the day ahead. How wonderful that Alyona was almost as excited about this wedding as her mother was herself. Madina had told her how she and Alyona had been meeting up regularly with Oleg over the months since the competition in Moscow, and how a special bond had already been growing between her daughter and her future husband. Just as well, since they'd all be living under one roof from next week onwards, after a short honeymoon period. Bela was so happy for them.

A couple of hours later, Bela, Madina, Alyona, Mama and Angelina were all having their hair and nails done at the local salon, along with Milana, who would be the other matron of honour. Bela was enjoying every moment of this pampering, and the others were all giggling happily too.

"You look happy, Alyona. I'm so glad," Madina said to her daughter.

"Of course, Mama. I'm happy for you, really I am."

"You're not disappointed that your father and I didn't work things out?"

"No. Not at all. You weren't really happy with Papa. I could see that. But when Oleg walks into the room you light up like the New Year tree in the main square on the thirty-first of December!"

Madina laughed. "I've grown to care so much for him over the past few months. He's a special man."

"And lucky to be marrying a wonderful woman like you." Alyona flashed her one of her famous smiles. "And even luckier to be getting such an amazing stepdaughter as myself, of course!"

"He won't know what's hit him!" Bela chimed in, and they all laughed.

The rest of the day went by in a blur, of course. The wedding was a small, private affair. Just a simple ceremony at the registry office, followed by a feast and dancing at Oleg's house on the outskirts of Shekala. Oleg's family had been very generous, and the long trestle tables were brimming with all sorts of dishes and delicacies. A local group were playing traditional Circassian music, with hand drums and accordions, and the guests were enjoying taking turns showing off their dancing skills inside the circle of onlookers. Everyone was clapping in time to the music and smiling. Bela was really enjoying herself. She couldn't think when she'd last had such a good time.

She watched as Oleg tenderly kissed his new bride on her forehead after they'd finished their dance in the middle of the circle. Yes, finally, Madina had found the happiness she'd been seeking for so long.

Azamat had been the next to dance, and Bela and Angelina had clapped loudly in time to the music. He was such a good dancer, what a shame he hadn't continued with the dance troupe he'd been a part of when he was younger. After the dance had finished, she watched him jog over to Milana and Alikhan and say a few words, before coming towards them.

"I'm off to get a drink, can I get you ladies anything?" he asked.

"Can I come with you, Uncle Azamat?" asked Angelina. "I'm thirsty."

"Of course, pumpkin."

"Can you get me a glass of water?" Bela asked.

"Of course," said Angelina, skipping off after Azamat. She seemed to be having a wonderful time too.

Bela noticed Alyona standing just a short distance away. She waved, and Alyona came over.

"Hi, Auntie Bela. Are you enjoying the party?"

"Yes, it's wonderful. I'm so happy for your mother. How does it feel to have a stepfather?" Bela asked.

"It feels good, actually. I like Oleg, he's a lot of fun."

Bela had been half wondering if Musa might turn up in a drunken state and crash the wedding, but so far there had been no sign of him. Hopefully he'd accepted Madina's choice and would leave her alone now.

"Alikhan's dancing skills are drawing much appreciation from the crowd," Bela observed, pointing with her chin towards the circle where it was now Alikhan's turn to shine. The boy had recently been introduced to his paternal grandparents, Aslan and Radima, and she herself had been able to get to know him a little the day before, when she'd helped Azamat go and find a wedding gift. Alikhan had come along with them, and Bela had taken to him immediately. He was a polite and well-mannered young man.

"Yes, he's an amazing dancer. I'm glad he and Uncle Azamat have been getting on well," said Alyona.

Angelina returned with a glass of water for Bela. It wasn't long before Alikhan's dance was finished, and he came over to join them.

"Alikhan, this is my cousin Angelina," said Alyona, introducing them. Bela noticed Angelina's cheeks reddening a little.

"I suppose then that we're cousins too," he said.

"Yes, but you're not related to this one," said Alyona, grinning. Poor Angelina's cheeks turned even redder.

"What's going on between Uncle Azamat and your mother?" Alyona was looking over towards the main house, and Alikhan and Bela both followed her gaze to the table where Azamat and Milana were chatting over a couple of drinks.

"Nothing. They're just friends."

"They look more than friends to me," said Alyona

"No, Azamat promised me. They won't get together unless I'm totally cool with it," replied Alikhan a little defensively.

"And are you?"

"What?"

"Cool with it? With the idea of them getting back together."

Alikhan thought for a moment. "I don't know. I need to think about it."

"Well, don't think about it too long. You want your mother to be happy, don't you? I think my uncle makes her happy," said Alyona.

"Alyona!" Bela warned. Sometimes her niece could be a little bit too direct.

Just at that moment, Alikhan's mother threw her head back and laughed at something Azamat had said.

"Well, someone's got to do the matchmaking around here. No time like the present!" Before he could object, Alyona had grabbed Alikhan's hand and was marching him off in the direction of his two biological parents. Bela sighed and watched them to see what would happen. She took a sip of the water and was glad to have a chair. She wasn't feeling quite herself today. All this travelling and excitement had been a bit much.

Chapter 33

Milana

Milana watched as Oleg kissed his new bride on the forehead after they'd finished their dance in the middle of the circle. It had been such a lovely wedding. As much as she genuinely wanted to be happy for her friend, she couldn't help but feel a stab of pain in her own heart. Would she ever move on like Madina had? Would she have another chance of happiness too?

Azamat was dancing now, and Milana couldn't take her eyes off him. She hadn't seen him dance since they were in that dance troupe together, years ago. Old memories came flooding back and her heart raced. He still had such an effect on her. Eventually the dance came to an end and Azamat directed his chosen partner back to the ring of onlookers and exited the dancing circle to give another man a chance to step up and choose a partner. He jogged over to where she and Alikhan were sitting, on the edge of one of the trestle tables. He panted a little, waiting to regain his breath.

"You should be proud of that performance, well

done," said Milana, hoping he couldn't hear the quiver in her voice.

"I still have it, then!" said Azamat, with a laugh. "I forgot how much I enjoy dancing. It's been a while since I've been at a wedding celebration, and I'm certainly having a great time at this one."

"Me too," said Milana, and she genuinely meant it.

"I'm off to get another drink," said Azamat. "Would you like anything?"

"Yes, some more wine would be lovely," said Milana, handing him her glass with a grateful smile.

"Alikhan?" asked Azamat. It was sweet of him to ask. He'd been trying so hard to get on well with Alikhan the past few months, and it finally looked as if Alikhan was warming up to him.

"Not for me. I feel inspired to take my turn in the ring," said Alikhan. He pushed his way through the crowd and was soon waiting for his chance to shine.

"I think you've set the bar quite high, and he wants to prove what he can do," joked Milana.

"I've no doubt he's a much better dancer than I ever was," said Azamat, a wistful look in his eye. "Right, I'll be back soon with your wine."

Azamat left her and went over to where Bela and Angelina were standing. Soon he and Angelina were heading into the main house. She noticed them returning a few minutes later. Angelina took a glass of water over to her mother, and Azamat brought a couple of wine glasses over to the table where she was still sitting.

"Did I miss Alikhan's dance?" asked Azamat, sitting down across from her, but with his body facing the dancers.

"No, look, he's about to start," she said. They both watched as her son strutted proudly around the circle, twisting and turning at just the right moments, his head held high and his arms rigid in the correct positions, one bent towards his chest, the other extended, fists clenched. She didn't recognise the lady he was dancing with, but she turned and glided around him before he finally guided her back towards the edge of the circle.

"Isn't he great?" said Milana, proudly. She wanted to add that Murat would have been so proud but swallowed her words before they came out. She didn't miss him so much anymore, but it was at moments like this when she felt sad that Murat would never get to watch his son grow up.

"He is," Azamat agreed. "And so much better than I ever was. Do you remember that time we were rehearsing for some big show? I was supposed to be spinning on my knees across the floor, and I lost control and spun right into the row of girls at the edge of the stage. I think I must have knocked over at least three of them."

Milana threw her head back and laughed. "Oh, my goodness, I'd forgotten about that. That was so funny. I nearly died laughing afterwards."

They carried on reminiscing about the past. It was fun to remember all the good times they'd shared growing up.

Just then, Alikhan approached with Alyona. Or rather, it looked like Alyona was dragging a rather reluctant Alikhan towards them.

"Alikhan has something he'd like to say," announced Alyona. Without offering an explanation, she gave Alikhan a wink and disappeared back into the crowd.

"What is it, sweetie?" Milana asked. "Is everything okay?"

"Um…"

"Alikhan?" What was going on now?

"I, um. I just wanted to say that… That if you two ever decide to get back together, then I'm cool with that."

There was a stunned silence.

Azamat coughed and cleared his throat. "Um, thank you. We appreciate that. That's, um, good to hear."

Alikhan looked pointedly at Milana and she felt her cheeks grow hot.

"I'll, um. I'll get back to the dancers," he muttered, and fled back to the safety of the crowd.

Milana's gaze followed her son back towards the dancers and musicians, her mouth opening and closing as if she wanted to say something but couldn't for the life of her think how to respond to what Alikhan had just said. It was cool if she and Azamat got back together? Where on earth had that come from?

"Are you okay?" Azamat's voice pulled her attention back to the conversation they'd just been having before Alikhan and Alyona burst in. What was it they were discussing? She couldn't remember now, but Azamat had made her laugh about something.

"Um… I… What was that about?"

"I think we've just been given Alikhan's blessing to become an item. If you want to of course?"

"I didn't know we were waiting for his blessing."

There was a pause. Milana frowned, feeling like she'd missed out on an important conversation somewhere along the line. "Do you want to fill me in?"

Azamat cleared his throat and brushed his hand through his hair. Then he looked deep into her eyes with that wonderful intensity of his that had captivated her when they'd first met. "You know that I never really stopped loving you, Milana. Not even after all those years. You were the only girl for me, you always will be."

Milana looked down at the glass in her hands, aware that her cheeks were burning. Azamat had loved her all this time? After what she did to him, taking his baby away and telling him not to see her again?

"I've behaved so badly towards you, I'm so sorry. I didn't really know what I was doing, but I know now that it wasn't fair to you. Can you forgive me?"

Azamat took her hand gently and kissed it. "Of course. Always."

"And you want to get back together?"

"Only if you're ready. I'll wait as long as I have to. I'm used to waiting!" He laughed, but behind the laugh there were years of pain. Milana was beginning to see that now.

"What did you say to Alikhan?"

"He was the one who brought it up. About four months ago. He told me he wasn't ready for us to get back together again. It was difficult enough trying to work out where I fitted in his life. I told him nothing would happen unless he was ready. I don't want to take the place of Murat. I know how much he meant to Alikhan. I didn't want him to think I was just taking advantage, you know? My relationship with Alikhan is so important to me, I didn't want to blow it."

"Oh, and do I get a say in any of this?" Milana laughed.

"Well, now's your time." Azamat laughed too. "What do you think? Are you ready to move on yet? Are you ready to move on with me?"

He suddenly looked terrified, like a rabbit caught in the glare of headlights, frozen, not knowing what was coming next. Milana had an overwhelming urge to give him a big hug and tell him everything was going to be okay, but then she glanced around at the wedding celebration. It wouldn't be appropriate, and this was an ideal place to start tongues wagging, which she was keen to avoid.

"I can't say I haven't thought about it," she admitted, her voice soft and low. "I guess... I don't know... It surprised me how much I missed Murat, once he was gone. But now..."

"But now...?"

She smiled at him, and it was as if years melted off her shoulders and they were seventeen again. "Now, I'm ready. I'm ready to give us another try. I think I'd like that very much."

"Me too." Azamat smiled back. "Me too."

Chapter 34

Bela

Mama was nervous, she could tell. And she didn't blame her. Bela had broken the news about Daniel two days after Madina's wedding. She'd been careful to do it when Papa was at work. It would be Mama's decision how much she would tell Aslan. At least Bela didn't have that burden weighing on her shoulders. This wasn't her secret so much as she was just the messenger. The one who had brought it to light after all these years.

She'd broken it to her as gently as possible, talking her through the story of what had happened since Mama had told her it had been a baby boy and not a baby girl, crushing her dreams of Irina being her long-lost sister. Little had she known at the time that her long-lost brother had been there, under her nose, all the while.

Of course, it wasn't totally unexpected. Mama admitted she'd had an inkling after meeting Daniel unexpectedly in the corridor of Lida's apartment. "There was something about him," she'd said. "Something familiar. But my mind just didn't want to go there. The pain was too deep, the memories too old and buried. I didn't allow myself to think about it. Just like I trained myself not to think about it when I gave him up."

"Are you okay about how things turned out, Mama? That Lida kept him and didn't tell you? You're not angry with her, are you?"

Mama thought for a while, and then sighed. "No, I'm not angry. I'd already decided to give him up, hadn't I? It wasn't my choice which family adopted him. Perhaps she could have tried harder to contact me, but I don't blame her. I deliberately avoided her calls all those years ago because I thought she would try to persuade me to take him back. I had no idea she was calling to tell me that she was the one who had adopted him. What a waste. All those years when I could have known about him, when I could have received news about how he was."

"Did you ever think about him, Mama?"

"Yes, of course, *lapochka*." Mama blinked back a tear. "A mother never forgets."

And so, Mama had flown back to Moscow with Bela, Michael and Angelina. She'd wanted to get it over and done with. Strike while the iron was hot. But Bela could tell that she was anxious about the meeting.

And finally, here they were, waiting outside Lida's apartment door, about to face the past. And the future.

Lida was the one who opened the door. "Radima. It's good to see you again." She gave Mama a big hug. "Come in, come in."

Bela had come bearing gifts from the Caucasus, but she left the bag in the hallway for now. Mama had taken off her coat and boots already, but was hanging back, obviously wanting Bela to walk into the living room first, ahead of her. Bela squeezed her mother's hand

and walked in with her. Daniel was standing there, waiting.

For what seemed like several minutes but must have just been a few seconds, Daniel and Mama just stood there, looking at each other. Everyone else hung back, anxiously, nervously. Willing this to go well.

Eventually, the two hugged, and when they pulled back, they both had tears in their eyes. Mama ran her hand down Daniel's face.

"You look so much like…"

"Like Azamat?" Daniel finished. "I know. I'm sorry I only met him very briefly last October. I can't wait to meet him properly."

The rest of the evening went so much better than Bela was expecting. Everyone loosened up, and soon the wine glasses were being refilled and everyone was joking and laughing. Daniel was his usual, charming, witty self, and Bela kept sneaking a glance at Mama, who seemed to be really taken with him.

"Lida did a good job, bringing him up," said Mama later, when they'd returned home. "He's turned into a charming young man. I don't think he would have turned out like that if I'd kept him."

"You don't mean that."

"Yes, yes I do. It was a shock at first, when you told me, but I can't think of anyone better I would have liked to adopt him. I never thought I'd see him again."

"Yes, that's true." Bela paused. "Do you regret giving him up?"

Mama shook her head. "No. I wasn't ready to have a child and be a single parent. At times I've felt terrible guilt and wondered what had happened to him, but now I know he's had a good life, a very good life, I have no regrets. And he's made Lida so happy. I knew how badly she and Vladimir wanted a baby. I don't know why I didn't think of the arrangement myself. I was just so desperate to get it all over and done with and get back home. I was young and naïve. Lida's been a much better mother."

Bela gave her a hug. "I think you've been a great mother."

Mama smiled. "I'm so happy I have you and Madina and Azamat. I don't deserve you all."

"Mama?"

"Yes?"

"I was just wondering. When you said that Daniel reminded you of someone, you didn't mean Azamat, did you?"

Mama shook her head and looked down at her lap. "No. He reminded me so much of his real father. I hadn't thought about him in years. It was so painful, the memory of what happened that night. I've no idea where he is now or what he's doing. It was just a silly flirtation that went wrong. Your father was the one I was really in love with."

"I know, Mama. I know."

Chapter 35

Azamat

There was only one place that would do as the perfect location for where he was going to propose. He'd known that all along, even while thinking up lots of different possible scenarios in his head. It had to be. The last bench just before the top of the hill in the park, overlooking the lake. It had been the very place where Milana had told him she was pregnant all those years ago, and suddenly their wonderful, exciting, passionate love affair had come to an end and they'd been forced by circumstances to grow up and become adults. And then this was the same place where she'd arranged to meet again to break his heart and tell him to give up any hope of ever seeing either her or his child again. This place represented so much pain in Azamat's life that he hadn't gone back to it again since that day, even though he'd walked in the park many times since. Even now, as he walked towards it, knowing that Milana would be meeting him there soon, he felt the blood draining out of his face and his hands trembling. His heart pounded in his chest, and his body was telling him to turn around and scamper back as quickly as he could.

He pressed forward, sticking his hands in his pockets and clenching his jaw. He needed to do this. He needed to redeem this place. He needed to confront the demons. He had a chance now to turn this small corner of the park into a place that represented love and joy in his life rather than heartbreak and anguish. It might seem silly to others, but to Azamat it made perfect sense. It would be as if he were erasing all those years, all those mistakes, and he'd have a chance for a fresh start. Both him and Milana. She didn't know it, but he had been going to ask her to marry him here all those years ago, when she told him she was keeping the baby. Now he would get to do it properly, and hopefully she would say yes.

His countenance lightened at the thought of Milana saying yes, and he relaxed his pace. Of course she was going to say yes, wasn't she?

Azamat's fingers touched something hard and metallic in his pocket. He turned it over and over, feeling the smooth edge of the gold ring and stroking the jagged edge of the single solitaire diamond on the top. It had been Bela's idea to propose with a ring. It wasn't really their custom here in the Caucasus, but things were changing now, becoming more Western. More American. Bela had convinced him that Milana would love it and she had even helped him pick it out. It had cost several months of his salary, but it would all be worth it if only she would say yes.

Was it too soon? It had only been two months since Madina and Oleg's wedding. Two months since Alikhan had given them his blessing and Milana had agreed to get back together. He'd been ready to marry her for years, but was she in the same place? Were they on the same page, or had he been reading her wrong? Oh well, he was about to find out. There was no turning back now.

There was the bench, just the same as it had been all those years ago, though perhaps with a fresh lick of paint. He walked on past it a short distance and stood at the crest of the hill, turning his eyes towards the café which overlooked the lake. Everything he'd planned seemed to be in place. His shoulders relaxed and he willed his heart to calm down and return to normal.

Footsteps. He turned his head, and there she was, coming towards him. She looked beautiful today. She always did, but today there was something even more special about her. Or was he just looking at her differently? His future bride? He walked back down towards the bench and met her there.

"Wow, I don't think I've been back here since..." her face fell as memories flooded back. He took her hand and guided her to sit down, next to him. "Me neither."

"Then what made you choose to meet here today?" The shadow had passed, and her eyes now glinted with happy curiosity.

"I wanted this bench to be a place not of painful memories but of happy ones instead."

"Oh?"

This was it. Keeping hold of her hand, he slid off the bench and knelt on one knee in front of her.

"Oh!" she said again, her lips curving into a coy smile.

"Milana, you know I love you with everything I am. You know I've never loved anyone but you. You light up my life like no-one or nothing else has ever been able to. You bring joy to my heart and you make everything in the world beautiful. I feel like God has moved so many mountains in the past few years, that have been standing in our way. Many of those mountains were my fault, and it seemed totally impossible to do anything about them. But now? It's like a miracle has happened. You, Alikhan. But especially you, Milana. The love of my life. And now that we've found each other again I never want to let you go." Azamat pulled the ring out of his pocket and held it towards her. "Milana, my love. Will you marry me?"

Milana took the ring, admired it, and slipped it on her finger. She looked at him, her eyes glistening with happy tears. "Yes, of course I'll marry you!"

Joy flooded into every fibre of Azamat's being, and he rose up, taking Milana in his arms. He wrapped his arms around her and brought his lips towards hers in a tender kiss. She slipped her arms around his body and drew him close. She was his, at last. He meant what he'd said, he would never, ever, let her go again.

Chapter 36

Bela

"Are they coming yet?" Angelina asked, straining to look around the pillar of the café in the direction Bela had implied was the correct one.

Bela had been excitedly looking in the same direction herself for several minutes. "Not yet. I'm sure they'll be here soon." She gave Michael a look that betrayed the nervousness she felt inside. What if...?

She'd helped Azamat plan this afternoon in great detail a few days ago and she so wanted everything to work out okay. "If not, we can always just carry on and have a lovely meal together anyway," she had assured him at the time.

"And I'll go home and slit my wrists," Azamat had replied, only half joking.

Bela looked over the table at Alikhan on the other side. There were two empty spaces saved beside him. She hadn't known the boy for long, but he seemed really sweet. In fact, she'd even caught Angelina sneaking shy glances at him, and she didn't blame her. She'd have done the same at her age.

"They're coming! They're coming!" Angelina stood up, nearly knocking over her chair in the process. The others at the table glanced up, each one a little anxiously. Madina, Oleg, Alyona, Alikhan. They were all here for what they hoped would be a celebration. But would there be something to celebrate?

"They're smiling, that's a good sign isn't it, *Tyotya* Bela?" whispered Angelina. Bela saw that, indeed, Azamat and Milana were radiating happiness as they walked hand in hand towards the café.

"Yes, that's definitely a good sign, *lapochka*. A very good sign indeed." Bela smiled and felt that her heart would burst. Everything was going to be okay. Things were finally turning out okay for everyone in her family. She glanced over at Madina and Oleg, who looked as if they were still on their honeymoon. They'd been married for two months now, and Bela couldn't be happier at Madina's choice of husband. He was a good man who'd finally treat her with the respect that she deserved.

Michael leaned over and whispered "Phew! I'm glad we didn't fly all the way down from Moscow for nothing." He grinned and she gave him a friendly jab in the stomach with her elbow. "What?" he objected playfully. "Twice in two months is a bit much, don't you think? Especially considering…" His hand went to her belly and he stroked the bump that was just becoming visible there.

Bela clasped her hand over his and leaned her head on his shoulder. If only she'd trusted God more at the beginning. There had been so many things that had seemed impossible; so many mountains that stood in the way of what she thought would make her happy. But God was a Mountain Mover, wasn't that what the song said?

She believed that now. So many wonderful things had happened in the last year. Yes, some terribly sad things too, but there was Madina happily married, and there was Azamat engaged to the love of his life at long last and reunited with the son he thought he'd lost. Bela smiled. When they were discussing the plans for the proposal, Azamat had asked her lots of questions about God and forgiveness. He was ready to know more, and Michael had already told him all about Jesus and how His death on the cross made it possible for anyone to be forgiven by God, no matter what they'd done in their past. But as Bela and Azamat had talked more deeply the other day, she could see that her brother was truly beginning to grasp the idea that God actually *wanted* to forgive him, despite the choices he'd made, and that there was nothing Azamat himself needed to do to earn that forgiveness. It was all paid for already, every bit.

Bela sighed and placed her hands on her belly, a feeling of utter contentment and love and gratitude filling up her soul. She lifted her eyes to the peaks of the mountains that were clearly visible now above the trees beyond the lake. She couldn't wait to tell this little one about the God who could move whole mountains, even ones as big as those she'd grown up with all her life, here in the Caucasus. Here in the place that would forever hold her heart.

Author's Note

I hope you enjoyed *He Can Move The Mountains*.

If you have a moment, I would be so grateful if you could leave a quick review on Amazon. Reviews help other readers to find the book and are especially important for independently published authors like myself. Thank you so much!

For book group discussion questions, local recipes, notifications of when new books are available, and so much more, sign up to join my Readers List at: www.catherinebarbey.com/readerslist

Acknowledgements

Writing a sequel to a novel was a lot more challenging than I was anticipating, and this second book has been more of a labour of love than the first. I want to express my gratitude to all those who encouraged me to keep going and to continue the story of Bela and her family. Thanks especially to my wonderful husband, who not only gave me time off from family duties in order to spend many hours tapping away on my keyboard in the local café, but who also did an amazing job of editing the book and finding cultural and grammatical errors that all but the keenest eye would have overlooked. My thanks also to my four lovely children, who inspire me daily.

Thanks to Sarah Furze and Sue Ricketts for your helpful feedback on my early draft, to Dr Fiona Thornton for information about sepsis, and to friends in Russia for their valuable insight and scrutiny of the final manuscript.

Thanks also to Rebecca Priestley, for your inspirational painting that became the cover for both of the books in this series, and to Rob Richards for your fantastic work, as always, on the cover design.

I appreciate so much the wonderful online community of independent authors, whose support and advice have been invaluable.

About the Author

Catherine Barbey writes Christian inspirational fiction
with an international flavour.
A tea drinking, home educating mother of four, she also
loves running and generally being outside in nature,
preferably in warm, foreign climes!
In a former life she worked alongside her husband in
linguistics and translation, living with her family in
Russia for eleven years. They are now settled back in
their home country of England, on the sunny south coast.

Catherine can be found blogging about her writing
journey at www.catherinebarbey.com

You can also connect with Catherine here:
facebook.com/catherinebarbeywriter

Printed in Poland
by Amazon Fulfillment
Poland Sp. z o.o., Wrocław

57742377R00148